D0826937

A
Harlequin
Romance

OTHER

Harlequin Romances

by ESSIE SUMMERS

Many of these titles are available at your local bookseller,
or through the Harlequin Reader Service.

For a free catalogue listing all available Harlequin Romances,
send your name and address to:

HARLEQUIN READER SERVICE,
M.P.O. Box 707, Niagara Falls, N.Y. 14302
Canadian address: Stratford, Ontario, Canada.

or use order coupon at back of book.

THE GOLD OF NOON

by

ESSIE SUMMERS

HARLEQUIN BOOKS   TORONTO
WINNIPEG

Original hard cover edition published in 1974
by Mills & Boon Limited.

© Essie Summers 1974

SBN 373-01884-3

Harlequin edition published June 1975

*All the characters in this book have no existence outside the
imagination of the Author, and have no relation whatsoever to
anyone bearing the same name or names. They are not even
distantly inspired by any individual known or unknown to the
Author, and all the incidents are pure invention.*

The Harlequin trade mark, consisting of the word
HARLEQUIN and the portrayal of a Harlequin, is registered
in the United States Patent Office and in the Canada Trade
Marks Office.

Printed in Canada

The Author records her thanks to the *Australian Woman's Mirror* for permission to quote Norma L. Davis's poem, *Hill-born*.

CHAPTER ONE

THERESA sat at a table under the chestnut trees of the restaurant garden at the top of the Kapuzinerberg in Salzburg, the letter from New Zealand in her hand, and knew this was the moment she had dreaded, when a clash of loyalties would eventuate . . . between New Zealand which was home, and Austria, the land of her ancestors, the country that had brought her healing when in anger and in bitterness she had cast Murdoch off.

Hardly knowing what she did, she dropped the letter on the table and the fingers of her right hand moved to caress, fleetingly, the place where once his emerald had lain.

Blessedly there were few tourists here, so she had the table to herself. It had been too hot, this August day, for many to attempt the climb to the Franziski Schloss. She could sit here to think it out, although she knew already that there was only one thing to do: go home. It was a thought unbearable that if she didn't she might never see Trudi again, old Trudi who had been a vital part of Theresa's life since babyhood. In everything except the ties of blood, the perfect grandmother.

Trudi, with her tales of Old Salzburg as it had been in the days of her short girlhood. Because Trudi had been barely eighteen when Archduke Francis Ferdinand had been assassinated at Sarajevo and the world had gone mad. By the time World War One had ended, that young, gay Trudi had been a widow, and not till a distant cousin of her neighbour's had come from New Zealand to look up the land of his ancestors, and had taken her back with him as his wife, and a mother to his children, away from the horror that was beginning to stir in Europe in the nineteen-thirties, had Trudi found happiness again.

There, in Central Otago, in the shadow of great

7

ranges that reminded her of her own dear mountains, in that place where a long-ago kinsman of her husband's had come to win a fortune from the fabulous goldfields of that area, Trudi had found a new family and home. Of all the members of that family, Trudi was the one most greatly loved and revered. She had always seemed ageless, indomitable, the type to live into the nineties, but now, at seventy-seven, this letter revealed that she was relinquishing her hold on life.

Perhaps a stranger reading this letter might not have guessed it was heralding the end of an era, but to anyone who had known energetic small Trudi, it was as certain as a death-knell. If the letter hadn't been enough, the fact that Theresa's mother had had to finish it confirmed her panic.

Trudi's letters had always been so full of the joy of life, the gratitude for the multitude of small things that had compensated her for her lopped-off girlhood, the fact that she had never borne a child of her own. She had loved New Zealand, a land so free, surrounded by relations who had filled the gap in her life, a terrible gap because none of her immediate family had survived that war. Trudi had built up a new tradition for herself, rejoicing in things rooted and established, dreading change, content always to stay in the shadow of her adopted mountains, revelling in the pioneer and goldmining history of her husband's family, linked so long ago with her own.

But now she was talking so casually of going into a home for the elderly. And not even in Queenstown, where Lake Wakatipu lay as bluely as any Austrian lake, where the Remarkables showed jagged peaks above the waters and dark pines serrated the edge of the sky where man had improved on nature; where sheep and cows grazed on hill pastures and the cycle of the years moved in ageless rhythm. She was saying: "I do not wish to be a burden to any of my dear ones, least of all to your mother, *Liebling,* who was surely the dearest step-daughter any woman could have had, and made a foreigner feel wanted and loved.

There is a very good home in Invercargill, and when a woman gets to my age, what does it matter where one lives? One needs only a good bed, a comfortable chair, a book to read at the day's end."

Only! Only that, *for Trudi!* Trudi, who, when Theresa had left home two years ago, was still milking the house-cows by hand, feeding her hens, tending her geese, tilling her vegetable garden, mending her own roof if no one stopped her. And Invercargill was *flat*. To think of Trudi living where not one mountain reared its height was unthinkable.

"Old Chess died a month ago. We buried him under the quince tree where he sat so often at my Emil's feet. I think the old dog would have liked that. But Ferdinand will have to be put down. Your mother would take him, but a cat is attached to his own place, always, and he would be so unhappy, for ever returning and being lonely and lost."

Trudi had continued her letter two days later. "Sorry I did not finish this, Maria Theresa. I couldn't be bothered that day. I lay down. The house was so dusty it worried me, but I was too tired to attempt to put it right. We had a high wind and your father had been using the tractor in the north field and this old dark furniture gets so coated. I ought to have had this house modernised long ago, it becomes a burden. But it will be a good site on which to build a fine new house for someone, I tell your father. Perhaps a modern house for a hired couple. I feel very tired, *Liebling*. I think I will leave this letter for your mother to finish. I suppose there will be items of news to tell you. I cannot think of any just now. My eyes are playing me up. Perhaps down in Invercargill they will get me some new glasses. I can't be bothered making an appointment in Queenstown. Give my love to your Tante Evelina and Uncle Ernst and Anton and" — Trudi's writing ended there and Theresa's mother had taken over.

"Tru went to sleep while writing this, Tess, and when she woke I didn't think she even knew she hadn't finished a sentence. I expect she was going to add: "to Nik and Peter and Anna". You'll guess by this she has quite suddenly aged. I think when she knew you were not, after all, going to marry Rudi, she lost interest in things. You were always so dear to her heart and she wanted happiness for you. Perhaps she was caught up with the romance of knowing you were going to marry a countryman of hers. She said: "The poor little one, first she jilted Murdoch, and now Rudolf has jilted her." In vain I tried to get her to recall that you'd said months ago the infatuation on your side hadn't lasted. But perhaps soon she'll forget that too. She's obviously slipping.

"But Tru is like a little bit of granite. I've asked the Home in Invercargill to defer her as long as possible — to place others before her. But I'm afraid that some day she'll just up and off. She wants to be no trouble to anyone.

"By the way, Murdoch's been in Canada some months. I think he intends teaching in England and Scotland later on. We heard about it in a letter from Geraldine, so perhaps she's told you. It's not so very far from where she's teaching. Well, about two hundred miles, but in a place the size of Canada that's practically next door. He'd gone over to see her. I must go. I'm sleeping across at Cloudy Hill every night, and must get over there before night comes on. It worries Tru. I'm sure that's why she put in her application for the Home. She thinks I ought to be home for Rod and the boys. Sometimes they come to Cloudy Hill for their dinner, but they prefer just to flop by their own hearth, so mostly I leave their meal ready to serve, in the oven. It's so cold for spring. How strange to think that where you are it will be unbearably hot. The other night I was late going over and Tru had dozed in her chair, the fire had gone out, and her hands were so white and cold. Must fly, love, Mother."

Theresa sat on with her chin in her hands, gazing into the distance. Presently she'd get herself some more coffee. She had never been going to marry Rudolf. Rudolf had been the son of Tante Evelina's neighbour and a ski instructor who'd come out for the winter season at Coronet Peak above Queenstown, that June. The June when she had found out about Murdoch. Rudolf had saved her face. He'd just been jilted himself, and they had pretended she had fallen in love with him and had gone to Salzburg with him and stayed with Tante Evelina, whose daughters were all married and who had been enchanted to have Theresa. She had tried to tell herself that she had got over loving Murdoch, that fresh scenes, fresh faces, and the adjustment problems of teaching in a foreign country had been all that was needed to take her mind off him.

She had loved teaching English and History and improving her German in this glorious city steeped in music and history, in culture and war and terror and delight, and she had filled her days with interesting things. Austria was so central. From here she had seen almost all of Europe. Most of the time she had been fairly happy even if — well, even if one no longer trod the heights. And love wasn't everything, she told herself fiercely.

Now Murdoch was no longer in New Zealand it would be so much easier to go home. But it meant she wouldn't fly there via Canada to see Geraldine. Trust Murdoch Gunn to be in the wrong place at the wrong time! Not content with snarling up her love-life, he'd snarled up her lifelong friendship with Geraldine too, so that life had become well and truly barren. Geraldine, who'd wept brokenly, when she'd told Theresa the truth about Murdoch. Geraldine had been very brave, and quite right. Far better, she'd said, to know before marriage than after. And yet, and yet — it had somehow taken something from the friendship. It wasn't fair to Geraldine. She suspected her friend had half feared this and had risked it nevertheless. But every time Theresa had seen Geraldine after that, she had flinched inwardly, as from a wound.

But lately she'd felt that after two years perhaps the old, sweet friendship might be resumed, that before long she might fly across in the school vacation, to be with Geraldine for a couple of weeks, to see the part of Canada she was in. But now Theresa knew she would not take the slightest risk of seeing Murdoch again. She would go home, but via Los Angeles, and across the Pacific.

She lifted her chin from her hands, pushed her thick honey-coloured hair from her ears — well, that was that. Decision made.

It was at that moment she heard it. The voice. A voice that said her name. Said it as no one else ever said it. But it *couldn't* be. Not *Murdoch's* voice, saying her name here on top of the Kapuzinerberg. Murdoch was supposed to be in Canada!

But he wasn't. He was here. He was somehow behind her and the owner of those footsteps she had heard and not recognised. His voice was saying: "Theresa? Maria Theresa?"

She didn't swing round suddenly as might have been expected. She froze into an unbelieving stillness. Then she turned slowly, as if on a heavy pivot. She knew the colour had left her face and hated herself for so revealing her feelings. But he *was* here, Murdoch, and her heart was behaving as it had always behaved, flooded with gladness, albeit a gladness shot through with pain.

In spite of it all, she managed a cool, casual greeting, "Good heavens — you! I was just reading a letter from home telling me you were in Canada, teaching."

"That's really out of date, though I was there, but just relieving. I was making my way here."

"Here? Austria? Or Europe in general?"

The dark reddish-brown eyes under the chestnut brows met hers and looked faintly amused. There was certainly no kindness in them. "You mean was my express purpose to seek you out? No."

Something hardened in Theresa. She met derision with derision. "My question wasn't meant to be personal. How vain can a man get! Languages are your specialty. I thought that, like me, you might have wanted to teach on the Continent, as distinct from most New Zealanders who come to the Northern Hemisphere but make a beeline for Britain."

"Oh, I've been here a month. Traversed the Danube fairly slowly, stayed in Vienna, revelling in the music, in the woods, and I spent a considerable time in Heiligenblut. You'll have gone there by now?"

Heiligenblut, with its legend of the Holy Blood that had given it its name, with the magnificent Grossglockner rearing its snowy heights above the flower-sprinkled meadows, the gay Austrian costumes, the utter peace of the little churchyard perched on the green hillside with its slender spire that was upflung above the valley but far below the mighty peaks that surrounded it . . . that churchyard with its endearing, intimate photographs of those who lay below set into their headstones. It seemed so fitting that they should sleep there, in their loved village.

She closed her eyes with the delight of remembering it. For a moment that hard crust softened. She opened her eyes, said, "It's of all places dearest to my heart."

His look was sharp, searching. "Would you say that back home? To your mother, for instance?" He added, as she did not immediately answer, "You used the superlative — 'dearest', you said."

Theresa managed a grin. "Always the schoolmaster — purist! Though we all do it. Tante Evelina sometimes teases me for speaking to her as if she were a small, naughty pupil!"

"You haven't answered me," he pointed out. "Is Heiligenblut as dear as Queenstown, as Arrowtown, as well loved as Cloudy Hill? Or Lake Iti-whakaata?"

Lake Iti-whakaata! The Lake of the Little Reflections. The Lake that reflected lilliput hills, tiny, gentle hills for an area that was rugged in the extreme but

13

for them. The lilliput lake where Murdoch had proposed to her on that long-ago day in the idyllic time when happiness was as natural as breathing and trust and confidence went hand-in-hand with them.

Even its name, uttered in Murdoch's New Zealand voice with its faint hint of a Scots burr underlining it, swept Theresa with an almost intolerable longing. But she managed to keep it out of her own voice and merely said lightly, "Oh, home is always the dearest and the best. I just meant Heiligenblut is my favourite place in Austria."

He nodded. "Very well. Now we'll have some coffee and something to eat."

"I mightn't want to eat. I could be slimming."

His eyes raked her, slim in a thin dress of yellow and green patterned silk, rather like sun shining through mimosa blooms, sleeveless and cool-looking, if anyone could be cool on a day like this. "You aren't slimming. You're already *too* thin. Imagine not eating after a climb like that! You'd need refuelling — what is it? Off your food? Well, I can understand it."

Colour, angry colour, stained Theresa's cheeks. "I get your meaning. You think what everyone else back home thinks — that Rudolf jilted me. He didn't. I always knew about Lisa. She was his first and only love. Rudolf and I were never engaged, never in love with each other. I danced very merrily at his wedding." She smacked at the letter lying on the table. "It's even in that letter, in Trudi's own words: 'The poor little one, jilted by Rudolf.' When he came to New Zealand, to the Peak, Rudolf and Lisa had quarrelled and parted. But there was never anyone else for him, and I knew from the start."

Murdoch took out his pipe, began to fill it. "I beg to differ, Theresa. Not always. Not at first. You were completely infatuated with him. That's why you broke it off with me, remember?"

Too late Theresa realised how her flash of temper had betrayed her. Her mind snatched wildly for some believable explanation.

14

Murdoch's match rasped, the little flame flared into life, outlined his profile for a heart-tugging moment, lit the tobacco, and a tiny curl of smoke ascended.

It was like incense to Theresa's nostrils. She said, snatching at a diversion, "Isn't that New Zealand tobacco? Surely you didn't bring a store that has lasted you till now?"

He laughed. "No. I travelled by air to Canada — no excess luggage. Murray Tynedale sent it over for my birthday. I hate to think what it cost in postage. Great kid, that. I'd said in a letter to Anita that I missed two things in England very much . . . pumpkins and my own tobacco. She said in reply that they could hardly freight pumpkins over, but Murray was sending some tobacco. I got it just before I left London for Munich."

Anita! The reason why, even if he still didn't know it, Theresa had broken their engagement.

She said, "How is Anita?"

"Very happy again. Nort came back to her, but not till Anita went to him and asked him to come back to them. I never dreamed she would, thought she'd have been too proud. I also thought Nort would have been too weak to hold out against her, till then. He took a risk leaving anyone as attractive as Anita on her own, though there's a lot more to her than just looks. She's also very wise — told Nort she just couldn't manage without him. They are very happy again now."

Theresa looked swiftly down. She couldn't bear to look at him. Who did he think he was kidding? Anyway, it had served to sidetrack his questioning. She was wrong about that; Murdoch said, "You haven't answered me. I said didn't you remember you broke it off with me because you were infatuated with Rudolf! So you just couldn't have known — always — that Lisa was his only love. Oh, I get it. You mean you always had doubts, knew you'd only caught him on the rebound? And when he went back to her, you stayed on here because you were too proud to admit it and go back home? Oh, well, I daresay it was awkward, with Rudi spending winters in N.Z."

This time she was careful not to get angry. But she didn't want, couldn't bear his pity. She didn't want to be a foolish ex-fiancée who had given up the substance for the shadow.

She laughed lightly. "Rudi was very sore about Lisa. They'd had a complete showdown. He asked me to pretend we were in love, to show Lisa he wasn't broken-hearted. *She* was the one who'd become — briefly — infatuated with someone else. Believe me, it gave her the most effective jolt when Rudi brought another girl back from N.Z. It looked really serious." She encountered a searching look from the eyes under the beetling brows. "It — it suited me well enough too, Murdoch. We'd talked a lot about things, Rudi and I. I — I just had to get away at that time. You see, that way we didn't have our entire circle of relations and friends trying to patch things up between us. They thought I'd fallen for someone else too."

His voice was very steady, but he'd transferred his gaze to look over the ancient wall to the high green hills beyond. "Let me get this straight. *Was* there anything — then — to patch up? We hadn't quarrelled."

She shook her head. "No. But I was looking for some way to break it off. Rudi had confided in me. I made a return confidence."

"Why? I mean why did you have to break it off? You'd better tell me, Theresa. I've a right to know why, if it wasn't that you'd imagined yourself in love with a glamorous ski-instructor, a man who was fit in every last detail, with the added charm of coming from the other side of the world."

She wouldn't give him the satisfaction of knowing she had suffered over him, had agonised over him, of how she had known of his deception. She wouldn't risk him guessing she still loved him, always would.

She said crisply, "But what a pity to drag it all up

again. That bit of deception on my part had served very well, I thought. We're both over it, long ago. I'd just drifted into that engagement to you, Murdoch. I hadn't had enough experience of life. You'd always been there. People thought it inevitable. I'd never had a chance to look round. Even at Teachers' College in Christchurch, you were teaching there. I'd hero-worshipped you as a kid — you know that. Later I mistook it for love. When I realised it wasn't I knew I must get away. You'd never have let me go if you'd known. You'd never have believed it was more than an early attack of pre-wedding nerves. So I took that way out."

There was a silence. Neither of them looked at the other. Then a wasp dive-bombed Theresa and she sprang up, overturning her chair. Murdoch made a swipe at it and it flew away. He picked up her chair, said abruptly, "I'll get us that coffee," and strode away across the courtyard, leaving her sitting there. She was as taut as a drumskin. Murdoch wouldn't leave it at that, she knew.

But he did. He came back with a tray, coffee-pot, cups and two plates, each holding an enormous slice of cake. He grinned as he set hers before her. "That ought to satisfy you, Tess. Remember when you were a kid you could never understand why cake with raisins and sultanas in it was called plum-cake? You thought there ought to be plums in it. That woman asked would I like plum-cake, and, heaven help us, produced this."

Theresa, grateful for his light tone, looked down to see a great wedge of a golden cake with cooked plums, burgundy red, set in the bottom of it. "It's one of their specialties here," she said.

Talk became general and the tension in her eased. She asked the usual questions mutual friends might ask of others back home. Though it seemed Murdoch hadn't been in Ludwigtown for some time. Perhaps because Nort was back with Anita? Murdoch had been Deputy Principal at a school in Queenstown when they had become engaged, but before that he'd spent all his holidays there, so that the friendship that had been almost lifelong as far as Theresa was concerned, had been a continuous one. His father had been rector of the Ludwigtown High School when Murdoch had been small and his parents had bought a weekend cottage beside Moana Kotare, on whose shores the small central Otago town nestled, when they had moved on. So Ludwigtown, named for Theresa's ancestor, was home to him too. Now he said, "Ah, that was good." Then he tapped the letter. "Was that the one that told you I was in Canada? — oh, it couldn't have been, I've been in England for weeks. That news would have reached you long since, I expect, from Geraldine?"

"I've not heard from Geraldine for months. My fault, really. I get so involved in other things here in Salzburg, I've little time for writing other than the family. But that news was in the letter. It was from Trudi — at least she began it, but Mother fin—"

She stopped as his hand went out to it, and he said, "May I read it?"

Quick as a flash her hand went out to cover the letter, to protect it from him.

He looked surprised. "I wasn't exactly going to snatch it. We almost always shared our letters from home, didn't we, in Christchurch? I've one here in my pocket from my mother if you'd like to read it."

Theresa had flushed a little. "It's — it's just that there's something in it I'd rather not share with anyone. It was—"

He shook his head impatiently. "You don't have to say why. I didn't mean to pry — simply thought it might be a usual run-of-the-mill small town letter. Your grandmother has the most vivid way of putting things — marvellous letter-writer. She kept on writing to me all the time I was at Oamaru, even after we parted, you and I. But I've got a lot of mail chasing me round at the moment, I think, and I've missed her letters. Trudi is so changeless. Makes you believe in stability."

She said slowly, "I'm afraid, Murdoch, that from that letter, time is at last catching up on Trudi. She began it but couldn't finish it. Mother had to. She — this may seem unbelievable to you — is thinking of going into a home for the elderly in Invercargill."

"What? Trudi? But it's unthinkable! She'd never want to leave the mountains. Has she had a stroke or something? Or are her faculties going?"

Theresa, to convince him, read him bits of the letter. Murdoch occasionally interjected sounds of incredulity. And he was silent for some time when she was done.

Even when he spoke he didn't utter the comforting words she expected. He said heavily, "I suppose it had to come. It does to us all, finally. A sudden failing, the mainspring slackening. Hard to realise for us, because we still know our usual vigour. Remember old Mrs. Mainwaring? The way she brought up that huge family on practically nothing. No one ever caught her wringing her hands and grizzling. Everyone vowed she'd live to be a hundred. Then when she was seventy-nine, the week after her grandson was ordained a minister of the kirk, she sat down, folded her hands in her lap and died."

Theresa stared at him, then said tartly, "Well, I must say you're a Job's comforter! You might've said this tiredness might not mean a thing; or that it might be temporary, the result of 'flu or something. Not that it was inevitably the beginning of the end!"

His voice had a rasp in it. "Oh, come, Theresa. You're not a little girl any more. I used to play it that way — yes. I had quite a few years on you and was apt to be too protective. But not any more. You're what? — Twenty-five? Time you grew up and faced facts. You can't expect to have the wind tempered to the shorn lamb always. Time is remorseless and doesn't pamper anyone."

Fury such as Theresa hadn't known for two years

19

and more rose up and swamped her. "You absolute prig! I never asked you to treat me that way, to protect me, shelter me. But you always did it. Maybe that's why I mistook affection for love — the sort of love that ought to exist between a man and a woman. I *do* face facts. I grew up very suddenly two years ago when I had the sense and the courage to admit I'd made a mistake and I broke our engagement. If that's not facing facts, what is?"

She found it maddening that he didn't flare up in return. He even laughed. She could have struck him. "Yes, I admit it is. Now I know the truth about why you broke the engagement — or what you *say* is the truth — I agree you did face facts then. But even so, you didn't strike out on your own. You accepted Rudolf's help, sought his protection, came over here to family connections, not strangers. And now you're all upset about this letter because it tells you things mightn't be the same when you go back home — if ever you do. You always want an alternative, don't you, Theresa? New scenes, new faces, someone to comfort you. Did it never occur to you that Trudi would grow old? That some day she might need her granddaughter living with her? She could have lived there a lot longer if you'd been there with her. She's not the sort to allow your mother to run two homes, year in, year out. If she's got that long!"

All sorts of emotions attacked Theresa — anger, pain, resentment, bewilderment. Murdoch had never spoken like this to her in his life. Even if he'd played her false with Anita, she'd never suspected him of mentally criticising her, finding fault. Had he always felt this way about her, had he had a certain reserve? Had he hoped she might mature, stop leaning upon him. Had he been glad, not sorry, when she'd broken the engagement?

Not that it meant he had, eventually, been able to marry Anita. Anita's husband had come back to her. *When* had he come back?

She looked up into Murdoch's face, so set, so

stern, so close to hers. And yet so far. "Murdoch, when did Anita's husband come back to her?"

The bewilderment on his face was almost comical. It was not often that Murdoch Gunn was at a loss for words. Then he said, "What on earth do you want to know that for — at this moment? What's it got to do with what we've just been talking about?"

She felt pleased. He'd expected her to be shattered by his strictures. Instead, it must now seem to him her thoughts had struck off at a tangent. Serve him right. That might take some of the wind out of his sails.

But he answered her question. "About the time you left New Zealand, I suppose. At least Mother said recently, in a letter, that she'd seen Anita, and said, 'I don't think that marriage will come unstuck again. Not after two years.' So it must have been about then. Yes, of course it was. A very good thing. Very bad for the children to have such divided loyalties."

(Yes, better for the children than a divorce and their mother to marry someone else. Murdoch would be like that, of course. He might have fallen under Anita's spell, but as a schoolteacher he'd seen so much of the effects of broken marriages on children's lives. Murdoch might have regrets about his own behaviour. She had a strong instinctive feeling that with Anita out of the way, now he knew she was not going to marry Rudolf, he was going to attempt to stir old ashes into leaping flame. Men were like that — thought they ought to settle down, after some sultry episode. Well, it was no use.)

He was watching her closely, she found. She didn't think he could possibly guess at her thoughts. She said, "Well, I told Tante Evelina that I'd be home by one for lunch. Would you like to come along some time and meet her?"

"I already have, and I'm expected back with you."

She dared not look put out. Instead she said, "It's a wonder, if you knew I was going home for lunch, that you just didn't wait down there till I came."

21

"Well, *you* climbed it, didn't you, Theresa?"

She said confusedly, embarrassed, "Yes, but—"

Murdoch reached out a big hand to hers, lying on the table.

"You wanted to get away from everybody, was that it? Taking to the heights as you always did, when you were bedevilled. Tess, did you come up here to lick your wounds alone?"

She said, "What wounds? I didn't come up here for any reason except that I wanted the exercise and this is one of my favourite rambles."

"Oh, don't fence with me, Tess. I know you too well. You were embarrassed just now. Why don't you just admit it? I didn't try to cover it up when *you* jilted *me*. I was always running into people who would ask when the wedding was going to be. Or would say, 'How's Theresa?' I simply used to say: 'Oh, she turned me down. She's in Austria. Met someone she liked better.' Doesn't it work that way with women? Like I said before, can't you face facts?"

Her eyes went a little cold, hard. In this light, under the dark brows that were so at variance with the light honey-coloured hair, they were more green than brown. She said levelly, "Well, if you're such a fact-facer yourself, perhaps you can face this one . . . it's a long climb on a hot day for anyone, much less a lame man."

He put his head back and roared. "Oh, Maria Theresa, you goose! I was never unduly sensitive about it. Besides—" He paused.

"Besides what?"

"You didn't recognise my footsteps, did you? Coming across the courtyard behind you?"

A line appeared between her brows. "No — but then though I'd have recognised them had I heard you behind me in Ludwigtown. I wasn't exactly expecting to hear them on top of a minor mountain in Salzburg, so — oh!" Realisation hit her as she recalled those footsteps. "Murdo, you *weren't* limping. Why? Oh—"

She wasn't aware she had used the old, loving diminutive of his name. She was staring at him. He pushed his chair back, rose, walked away from her to the ancient wall that rimmed the courtyard of the schloss, and stood there for a long moment looking out over the incredibly green countryside dotted with farms and monasteries and convents. Then he walked back to her, smiling.

He had no trace of a limp left.

Constraint was gone. Theresa's eyes were warm again, a-sparkle.

"How magnificent. But how? And why did no one tell me?"

"No idea. It was a very clever surgeon in Oamaru. He'd been studying over here a few years, and as a mountaineer himself, took a post here and had great experience in mountaineering accidents. It was a complicated sort of thing, but recent research had thrown new light upon it, and I was so fit in general health, it was one hundred per cent successful. In a year's time I ought to be able to ski again."

Theresa made a waving-away gesture. "Oh, that doesn't matter! In fact I'd hate to think of you risking it. What really matters is that you can run again. I guess you enjoyed cricket more again when you got over that injury. It wasn't much fun having someone to run for you, was it?"

A strange look glimmered in his eyes for a moment and was gone.

"Skiing was the thing I did with you. Cricket wasn't. And in Austria it's more important.

"But cricket was your ruling passion." Then she added: "Did you really think I'd be gladder about the skiing? Then you *must* think me selfish!"

He didn't beg her pardon, merely said again, "Well, skiing's more useful here. It'll be some time before I handle a cricket bat again."

She said slowly, "Then you really do mean to stay for a time? Teach here? Spend the winter season?"

"Yes, why not? Know of any openings?"

23

"Not at the moment. But you could make enquiries."
She decided to switch the conversation. "Where are you staying?"

"At the Pension Doktorwirt at Salzburg Aigen. Though your aunt immediately suggested that now Anton is married, I could stay with them. No objection to that, I suppose?"

Her tone was as nonchalant as his. "No, of course not. You'll enjoy Tante Evelina's cooking. Her apfelstrudel and her wiener schnitzels are superb and her home-made wines and sausages are out of this world." She must not show she dreaded the thought of living at such close quarters with him.

"Good. By the way, she said this letter from home had just come for you." He took it out of the hip pocket of his shorts and flipped it on to the table.

She said, with quick dread, "Another — so soon — oh, I hope—"

"Oh, sorry. Not bad news, because it's not from the Ridge or Cloudy Hill. I noticed the address on the back. It's from Gwenda Lloyd, look!" He turned it over. "I oughtn't to have used the word home. I only meant from Ludwigtown. Gwenda still secretary at the school?"

"Yes, she writes regularly. Her letters are such fun. That way I keep up with all the school gossip, staff and pupils alike, and so on. Do you mind if I read it?"

She slit open the envelope with her teaspoon handle. It wasn't as fat a letter as usual, but an enclosure fell out. She looked at it quickly and curiously, turned it over and, as the heading met her gaze, almost exclaimed aloud, but with an automatic reaction, slipped it, still folded, into the breast pocket of her dress. It was — of all things — an Education Board Application Form. What on earth was Gwenda Lloyd up to?

She soon found out and had to stifle an impulse to move away out of possible range of Murdoch's sight. Gwenda had come to the point quickly. One of the teachers had had to leave suddenly because of family illness. They would be needing someone for

German, English and some History. Didn't she ever want to come back home? If so, and it was time she did, after gallivanting about the world for two years, the job was tailor-made for her. No guarantee she'd get it of course, but she thought there'd be no harm mentioning it and as time was short, had put in the form.

These classes would suit Theresa down to the ground, she was sure, and she'd write more another time, but she wanted to get this letter away pronto in case Tess might consider it. 'I know you must have had a wonderful time, Tess, and every time I read a letter from you I get itchy feet myself, but even so, at times you must experience a great *haraeth*. Of course I am quite mad, when I think of the extraordinary adventures you used to involve *me* in, even, much less the rest of the staff, but perhaps absence does have an affect on the emotions. However, there could be worse than you — and better the devil you know than the devil you don't, I say.' *Haraeth?* Some Welsh word? Gwenda had been a Richards before she married a fellow Welshman and often used the odd Welsh word, but she hadn't heard that one before as far as she remembered. Theresa looked up to meet Murdoch's gaze. She said, "Do you know any Welsh?"

"A few words, no more. From my reading. I'm more familiar with the Gaelic, from Grandfather. What word are you after?"

"*Haraeth*."

"Ah, a pretty word. It means, I think, nostalgia. The homesickness of the heart. Does that fit the context?"

"Yes. I think she wants to know am I ever homesick for the gorges and the lakes."

"And are you?"

"Yes. I think I'll go home soon."

He showed instant aversion to the idea. "As soon as I've come? That's pretty poor."

Theresa looked down, fiddled with folding the

letter, said, "Oh, I'll show you round in the next week or two. If I don't go back to my teaching post when school resumes, it could be an opening for you. I rather think I'm going to be needed at Cloudy Hill. Trudi wouldn't go to Invercargill if I was there with her. You said that yourself."

"So I did." His face was rather grim.

They rose, threaded their way back down the steps by the crumbling wall, grateful for the shade of incredibly ancient trees. They forsook the lower path to wander downhill through leafy glades, glad of small talk about all that lay about them, enchanting the eye, wooing the other senses with spicy woodsy odours and the sound of bird-calls. They stopped now and then to examine the carvings in wood that told them the names of the trees.

Once Murdoch caught at her swiftly, his arm about her, to hush her into silence and stillness as he caught sight of deer grazing. It was almost more than Theresa could bear, his closeness, but in a moment or two he released her. They came out onto the main path that wound down by the old monastery and would presently take them to the riverside and stopped, spellbound, as, perfectly framed in a gap in the trees, they saw the fortress, rearing up above the Salzbach River, almost three hundred feet high, where, eleven hundred years ago, Saint Erentrudis had built her "castle of God".

It had a fairy-tale quality, truly a castle of dreams. Below it clustered buildings steeped in tradition, in legend, in history . . . in convent roofs, cathedral roofs, verdigris green overlying their bronze. Trees were everywhere, to give shade and coolness to tourists and residents alike, trees under which the child Mozart must have played, played and listened.

That same magic quivered in Theresa's pulses. She was here, with Murdo, leaning on this wall that had heard so many secrets, had known so many footsteps passing by, or pausing. Life was like that. Even if it denied you more lasting joys, there were the small bonuses, moments you would remember all your life long. Soon she would be on the other side of the world, and Murdo would be here, and sometimes when she looked across the Arrow River into the dark and lonely gorge, she would remember this hot, bright day, shared with him, in the Old World, and looking at the sharp crags on the heights of a land that was called Down Under, there would be a mist before her eyes and she would imagine she saw the fairy-tale fortress of Salzburg.

"Not a cloud in the sky," said Murdoch.

Theresa didn't reply because her eyes had misted over and the castle was dancing before her vision as if it had been diamonded with dew, or, as she had so often seen it, blindingly crystallised with snow, under winter sunlight.

Then she gave herself a mental shake, told herself sternly: "Don't for Pete's sake go all dewy-eyed and sentimental over him again. He isn't worth it. He deceived you once, he could again. Women are fools who think men will reform after marriage. Just as well you've decided to go home. He's so dominantly male, so sure he's right, and, like all the Gunn clan, ruthless. His second name isn't Olave for nothing. The Gunns never did bring the Keiths anything but sorrow."

They walked down the cobbled streets and twisting lanes of the shopping area this side of the river, then up a little street to where Ernst, Tante Evelina's husband, sold his leather goods and his beaten brass wall plaques to throngs of tourists. They went in by the side door on the street, up the narrow stairs into the dim coolness of the old, old house that was next door to the one where Trudi had spent her long-ago girlhood.

Tante Evelina was stirring her soup-pot. Yes, even on a day like this, there would be soup. But first she gave them some deliciously cold blackcurrant juice to quench their thirst. She was beaming on them as if Murdoch's coming was all that had been needed to set a crown upon the summer's happiness. With great misgiving, Theresa recognised the matchmaking gleam in her eye.

CHAPTER TWO

SHE HAD further misgivings when she saw what a success Murdoch was with the family. Tante Evelina approved his appetite, his physique, lean to the point of hardness, yet broad and well-nourished, she said, making him chuckle, his reasonable fluency in the German language, his good common sense in not being too independent, in accepting her offer of hospitality. Uncle Ernst approved him for the most part in silence, but Theresa could tell it was approval, sitting in the corner, smoking a pipe with him, nodding now and then and observing him with shrewd kindliness.

Theresa decided that soon she would leave them to it, plead letters to write, say she was going to have an early night. She had found the long afternoon a strain. She would read both letters again in the privacy of her room, though she knew she would go home soon whether or not she obtained that position. She'd saved a good deal while living here and she could merely housekeep for her step-grandmamma without desperately needing a job.

Before she could excuse herself, Murdoch stopped talking about New Zealand and said to her, "Come on over to my hotel with me, Theresa. The Doktorwirt does a really good Salzburger Nockerl — I shared one last night with one of the girls in a tourist party — and I ordered one for ten tonight for you and me."

Theresa said crossly, "You took a long chance on that, didn't you! I could have been tied up tonight. I just don't stay home and sit in my corner every night, you know."

Uncle Ernst peered over his steel-rimmed glasses at her. "Have you been out too long in the sun today, little one? Are you tired and — what is that word you use I like so much? tired and crotchety? That was quite ungracious when this young man has just arrived here and has planned this pleasure for you."

29

Murdoch burst out laughing. "It's Kiwi frankness, that's all, Uncle Ernst. That, and the fact we've known each other all our lives. Sorry about that, Tess. Will you come, if you aren't breaking a date?"

"A date?" pondered Tante Evelina. "Breaking a date. Is that like Theresa says sometimes, that she wishes to pick a bone with someone? Theresa, you will not quarrel, I hope, on Murdoch's first night!"

Murdoch shook his head. "I shan't allow her to. And it doesn't mean that. It means I ought to have asked her first, if any other young man was going to take her to share a Nockerl, or drink wine with him, or take her to some chamber music. Theresa, are you entirely free and will you come?"

Theresa was brooding darkly on the fact that he'd called *her* kinsman *uncle*. What a nerve! She said reluctantly, "Well, I had meant to write a letter, but—"

Tante Evelina beamed. "But you will run upstairs and brush your beautiful hair and put on your green and red frock and Murdoch will be so proud of you at the Doktorwirt."

Murdoch laughed. "Tante, you would please my father. Because you're Austrian, you pronounce Murdoch as it should be pronounced. The ch in both languages is the same. The Sassenachs give it a k sound."

Theresa turned at the door. "Murdoch and his father, and all the Gunns I know, are throwbacks."

Tante Evelina looked bewildered. "Trowbacks . . . what are trowbacks? It is word I do not know."

Theresa looked mock-serious and said it in German. "It means they retain the qualities of their ancestors, good and bad. And Clan Gunn was noted for its warlike and ferocious characters. *And* they happened to be the traditional enemies of my father's people, the Keiths. Murdoch there even bears the name of his mighty and fearful ancestor, Olave the Black, Norse King of Man and the Isles." A mischievous glint gleamed greenly in her eyes. "It makes him dictatorial."

Murdoch answered in the same language, though naturally much slower than Theresa, "Aye, we were warlike and ferocious, I grant you, but there was one thing about us — we never attacked our enemies when they were at prayer! We left that to the Keiths. And you would do well, Theresa Keith, to remember some day that your clan motto is: 'Truth conquers.' " For a moment they had an eyeball-to-eyeball encounter and the mischief died right out of Theresa's eyes. She went slowly and thoughtfully upstairs. Murdoch had not, then, believed she had given him up because she had found out she no longer loved him. She must walk warily these last few days in Austria. She had only her pride left, the pride that when she found out she had lost Murdoch to Anita had been all that had sustained her.

Did it mean he still thought she *had* been infatuated with Rudolf? And had been jilted? That rather stung. Or did he suspect there was some other reason, and was here to find it out? Either way, she didn't like it. But what matter? In a few days she would be on her way home, and Murdoch would be left in Salzburg.

She'd better not disappoint Tante Evelina about her dress. It wasn't national dress, but had the hint of it in the black waist-yoke in a modified form, the lacing, the red and the green of it, the frill of white embroidery at the deep, square-cut neckline. But Theresa got into it quickly and did not spend too long brushing out the thick curving sweep of her honey-coloured hair. Her make-up went on speedily too. Then she sat down at her small table under the eave, filled in the application form, slipped it into an airmail envelope, attached the stamp. She slid it into a reticule bag of soft chamois, drew the strings and ran lightly down the stairs, like any girl eager for an outing.

Just as she entered a bell rang, an old-fashioned one, from a pull on the street door. Uncle Ernst went down and presently two young people were running ahead

31

of him up the stairs and into the dim old room, Rudolf and Lisa, back from their prolonged honeymoon in New Zealand, for the snow sports season, where Rudolf, as usual, had been an instructor.

Rudolf seized Theresa, twirled her round, kissed her lightly on both cheeks, was pushed aside by Lisa who did the same. "One kiss is from your mother, Theresa, one from your grandmamma."

"But we didn't expect you yet," Theresa was stammering.

"*Ach* no, but it was an early snow season, and it ended early too. The championships, they are all over, and the thaw has set in. We wanted to be home, to have a touch of autumn before we have another winter upon us. Next month the trees here will be turning golden. Oh, but I loved your New Zealand, Theresa. Some day, I hope, Rudi will take me back there in summer. I don't want to know it only in winter." She paused, suddenly aware of a stranger in the corner now her eyes were becoming used to the dimness.

Ernst moved to the wall, switched on the centre light. Evelina spoke very clearly. "It is Murdoch Gunn, also from Ludwigtown, Lisa. He just arrived today."

Lisa didn't connect the name with the man Theresa had once been engaged to, however. She was bubbling over with happiness. She said, "How lovely for Theresa to have someone from home here. I am so glad for her. Sometimes I have thought she must have been homesick for a known and familiar face, even though we have all loved her and we never want her to go away. As for me—" she looked directly up into Murdoch's face — "I even owe her my present happiness, my marriage. I was a very foolish girl. I quarrelled with Rudi. I even thought I was in love with some other man. But when he came back from New Zealand with another girl, and I thought I had lost him, then I knew he was the only man I would ever want to marry. And what do you think? They were just pretending! Wasn't it clever of Rudi? He planned the whole thing. And I had thought him unromantic! Tak-

32

ing me too much for granted. But he did all that for me. And Theresa was a — what is it you say? — a good sport? And even then Rudolf would not marry me right away — he said I was to be sure, this time."

Rudolf's face was a study. He and Murdoch had met before. He put his arm round Lisa's shoulders very quickly, said to Murdoch, "Do forgive my little babbling brook. She is a little intoxicated with the joy of being back home, I think. Nice to have you here, Murdoch."

Even then Lisa didn't tumble to it. She said, "Oh, you already know Murdoch, Rudi? How nice. You met him on a previous visit?"

Murdoch said, "We saw quite a lot of each other, really. My people lived in Ludwigtown for years, so I spend a lot of holidays there. My father was the rector of the High School. Theresa taught there after she finished her training. I used to stay with her step-grandmamma sometimes, if the lake cottage my people had was let to tenants."

Lisa said, "Oh, Trudi? She was so sweet to me. She is a wonderful person. One just cannot believe she is in her seventies."

Murdoch said, rather quickly, "Unfortunately, she's had a setback, and is losing grip a little. Theresa had word about it today."

Rudolf made an incredulous sound and Theresa turned to him, began to say, "Hard to believe, isn't it, but—" and was aware he was not attending to her, but staring at Murdoch, over her head. At least so she thought. But he dropped his gaze to her, said, "Yes, hard to believe, but then that's the way of it. So little indication outwardly, but I think it's due to tiny haemorrhages, pinpoint ones in the brain, allied in a very small way to strokes. But what a gloomy conversation! Trudi would be the first to scold us, would say this has been the way of all flesh from the beginning and that she has lived her life. If Murdoch has just arrived, we must celebrate. We must go out somewhere together."

Murdoch said, "Theresa and I have a table booked at the Doktorwirt — a very modest celebration, just a bottle of wine and a Salzburger Nockerl. Would you care to join us? I could ring to order another. Or perhaps you would? My German is rather of the schoolroom kind, not nearly as fluent as Theresa's."

They came out to an enchanted evening and a fairy tale city with, across the river, the fortress castle bathed in an unearthly green light that seemed to float it among the stars like a castle in the air, and below it the Cathedral roofs were floodlit in white, and golden and rosy glows outlined other buildings.

They came down cobbled streets and suddenly Theresa said, "Wait for me here a moment, I have to post a letter," and slipped away from them. She felt a decision had been signed and sealed when she heard it plop.

She thought the other three cut off their low-voiced conversation very abruptly when she returned to them. She hoped Lisa wasn't asking Murdoch what might be embarrassing questions. She mustn't leave them alone again. But surely by now Rudolf would have whispered to his wife that Murdoch was the man to whom Theresa had once been engaged?

There was a tantalising delight in walking with Murdoch in this fascinating city. Salzburg, at night, in August, had a gaiety and excitement all its own. Almost everyone in the street had anticipation mirrored in their eyes . . . Festival time, and there would be music in the squares. The fountains would sing their ceaseless songs, the droplets upflung to catch the silver reflections of the stars, people would pace the cobbles in leisurely fashion, women were gowned to suit the occasion, in Austrian peasant fashion, or in long, graceful dresses, with filmy stoles about their shoulders, necklaces sparkling, earrings swinging.

They crossed the bridge, turned left, went across

the road to wait for the bus. Murdoch laughed. "I'm still not orientated to this driving on the right. I feel we ought to be waiting on the other side by the river."

Presently they had left the bus and were walking along the quiet, flower-bordered lane that led to the Doktorwirt. "Listen," Murdoch said, and they stopped. From inside a house came the sounds of someone playing on the piano, "My Favourite Things" from *The Sound of Music*.

"How right and proper," he said, "in this suburb where the Trapp family lived."

Rudolf said, smiling, "I thought *we* would have been telling *you* these things. It sounds to me as if you have come in the ideal tourist way, Murdoch, armed with knowledge. I expect you know our history, too, as well, if not better, than we do ourselves."

Murdoch grinned, "Well, I teach history. And of course, living in Ludwigtown, we knew more about Austria than any other European country. We did a lot of studying together on it, didn't we, Tess? In Trudi's attic, during holidays. Trudi used to join us, to add her own tales to the legends and facts we unearthed. We knew a lot about Maria Theresa, of course, and what an enlightened ruler she was, for her day and generation. I expect you know that Theresa here was named for her. I could scarcely believe I was seeing her palace for myself when I went through the Schloss Schonbrunn in Vienna. Did you see it, Theresa?"

Pain, from past remembered sweetnesses, jabbed Theresa. Yes, she had seen it, alone. Not with Murdoch. In imagination and desire she was back in that attic room, built to Austrian design by a long-ago ancestor, with the little windows flung wide to the wind that came whistling through the Gorge.

Down below her father and Joe, who was really Josef, and Bill, who was Wilhelm, were trying to match motherless lambs with lambless ewes and being patient with Brenda, their little sister, who was more hindrance than help. Theresa's grandfather, Emil, was gathering daffodils from under the orchard trees, for Trudi. And Theresa could hear Murdoch saying, from over the bridge of the years, "Some day I'll take her there, Trudi, to see it all for herself. And we'll go to the Mirabell Gardens to hear chamber music as you used to do, and we'll think of you and this night, when we planned to do it."

They had both seen it, yes, but separately. The bitter-sweetness of that memory was almost too poignant to be borne. Theresa was glad to go inside from the flower-scented night, into the friendly, wood-panelled atmosphere of the Doktorwirt, with its wooden pews grouped round the tables.

There was singing, of course, incomparably spontaneous and gay singing, with some of them keeping time rhythmically with the base of beer steins on the wooden table, then an elderly man with a nutcracker face, seamed and brown, and looking exactly like the wood-carving profiles Uncle Ernst sold in his shop, came in with his concertina and began to play a Strauss waltz. There was very little room, but they danced between the benches, laughing, gay.

It had been a long time since Theresa had been in Murdoch's arms and she had difficulty in reminding herself that it didn't have the meaning it once had. It was so alike, yet so different. His cheek wasn't against her hair as once, his handclasp was light, impersonal, and he held her no closer than he'd have held any partner. But it was still heaven for a little while.

They wandered out to the patio to cool off and watched the lucky bathers in the lit pool. Above them the mountains and hills circled them round and laughter and happy voices added their own enchantment to the night of blue-velvet sky and silver sequin stars.

Murdoch excused himself, came back, said, "I've managed to borrow bathing suits for you. I've got mine here, of course. How about it?"

It was irresistible. Lisa said, "You are like a conjuror — producing bathing-suits like that — how do you do it?"

There was an edge to Theresa's tone. "It's his fatal charm. No doubt the women in that tour party just about fell over themselves to lend him what he asked for. It smooths Murdoch's path for him times without number. It's never been known to fail."

"Oh, there *was* the exception that proved the rule," said Murdoch suavely.

There was an awkward silence. Theresa could have bitten her tongue out. What a fool she was!

Then Rudolf said, "Well, you girls go up to Murdoch's room first — and don't be long. The moment Murdoch mentioned bathing, the heat became unbearable. Lisa, can you credit that two weeks ago we were cleaning snow off our skis?"

Theresa had a fleeting thought that if they'd been at Coronet Peak just two weeks ago, then Trudi's capitulation to age must have been very sudden indeed. She'd imagined they had left earlier.

Lisa laughed, said, "Quite incredible. I'll just pin my plaits on top of my head and won't dive. How about you, Theresa?"

She shook her head, the thick light hair with its darker glints showing beneath the top strands swinging from side to side. "I still love the feel of the water rushing through my hair against my scalp, and for some reason, mine dries very quickly."

She came out in a purple two-piece bathing-suit with a scalloped line below the bra with embroidered eyelet holes in it.

"That's very fetching," said Murdoch, surveying her in the corridor, "it would make a very intriguing pattern of suntan, I'd say."

Theresa felt stupidly breathless, and found it hard to reply naturally, but managed, "Just as well we're bathing by moonlight."

"Well, starlight. There isn't a moon."

Theresa decided that the way her heart was behaving it was just as well there wasn't. Murdoch and moonlight had always proved a strong alchemy. There was but one thing to do, cut and run. Austria, and especially Salzburg, were places too romantic by far. Mountains and moons, chamber music and Strauss evenings, lakes and waterfalls, cobbled streets where moonlight slanted bewitching shadows and where you had to walk close; scents and little zephyrs, and the exquisite grace and symmetry of buildings designed by architects who knew how to erect poems in stone, and raised by builders who were master-craftsmen. Oh, no, she mustn't stay in Austria now Murdo was here!

She caught Lisa's hand, and ran lightly down the stairs and out to the pool, lifted her arms above her head and dived into the deliciously cool depths, coming up to find Murdoch surfacing beside her. There were fewer than a dozen in the pool now, all in frolicsome mood. They gambolled like dolphins, luxuriating in the matchless feel of dark water against hot skin, the caress of a gentle zephyr against wet cheeks.

Through it all Theresa was conscious of gratitude because here, in contrast to the glaring light of day, she could, in this friendly darkness, occasionally study Murdoch's features. Features that were, in any case, etched on her memory for all time, but it gave her exquisite pleasure to be looking on them once more. Aquiline nose above lips that could be so stern but could relax instantly and often into uncontrollable laughter. His dark chestnut hair, wiry, rather aggressive-looking, sprang from a broad brow, he had a tanned skin, eyes that looked almost black but were reddish-brown in a strong light, and a square, good-natured but indomitable chin . . . the chin that Theresa had so often kissed. She shivered suddenly.

"Come back, Tess," said Murdoch's voice in her ear. "Where are you . . . gazing into space like that?" His voice roughened a little. "Are you back in New Zealand?"

"Yes, beside the Awhitu."

38

She thought his jaw tightened. "Must you? Yearn for New Zealand the moment I arrive?"

She shrugged. "It's not sudden. I've had moments of homesickness many times. Sometimes I feel like an immigrant must. I've got a divided heart. I love Salzburg so much. Perhaps it's these racial memories they talk about. It's the home of my forebears. Sometimes I feel as they said Anna always felt, as if a little bit of her heart would always be Austria's. So much of her love for it would have to be hidden away during World War One when feelings ran so high. She was a very old lady then, and a sad one, they said. But wasn't it wonderful that she lived long enough to see her grandson bring Trudi to Ludwigtown? They all seemed so long-lived I thought Trudi would have been the same."

He said gently, "It doesn't always follow. Yet I too have always thought that about Trudi. This change must be very sudden. Only——"

He seemed reluctant to finish his sentence — then, when she prompted him, did. "Only sometimes people last a long time, not ageing. But if they suddenly realise they must transplant themselves, they give up in spirit."

"That's what I think," said Theresa firmly. "It mustn't be allowed to happen to Trudi." She called to Lisa, back in the pool, "Let's go up now and get into our clothes."

It was better to bring this evening to a close, to remember her responsibilities. By day, the enchantment would vanish before the harsh light of day. She mustn't be weak. She knew only too well that Murdo had the power to blind her to his own weaknesses. And that was one weakness she could not, would not, tolerate — unfaithfulness.

When Tante Evelina woke Theresa the next morning, she saw traces of tears on her cheeks, tears Theresa, unknowingly, had shed in her sleep. So Tante did not draw the curtains back, she left them as they

39

were, only the revealing shaft of light striking between them as they stirred in the breeze.

"Another hot day, *Liebling*, but a beautiful one. After Murdoch comes this afternoon with his baggage, you should wait for evening before you go for a stroll, I think. He said it would not be till well on in the afternoon, anyway. He is going with a party from the pension up the Untersberg this morning. He said to me you would have been there often." So she had, but — oh, how stupid could one be? He'd be very happy, no doubt, with that attractive girl from Canada who'd loaned him the purple swimsuit. Murdoch wouldn't lack feminine company, ever. From *Canada*. H'mm. Was it possible he had met her there, and tagged along after her? Was it possible Theresa was deluding herself imagining he wanted to blow new life into old ashes? Anyway, none of it mattered because in any case she was going to cut and run. Not that she was fleeing from her own tumultuous feelings. Of course not. It was Trudi's need that mattered. Trudi who was actually considering leaving all she had loved so long. There was that poem Trudi had loved, the one a small Theresa had copied into her first scrapbook. But she wouldn't read it over now. She didn't need that to spur her on. She'd taken the first step yesterday night when she had filled in that application form and posted it off.

This morning with Murdoch safely up the Untersberg she would go down into the town and book herself a flight from Munich to London Airport, and from Heathrow to New Zealand. She'd have liked a day or two in which to say goodbye to London, which she had so dearly loved, but she dared not linger too long, because time might run out for Trudi.

It was all so easy. Travel clerks were so casually efficient. It was just another booking to them, yet decisions that could affect Theresa's whole life were in that little slip of paper. The fact she was still within the time-limit for her smallpox vaccination helped.

The confirmations would be back quite soon. When Theresa came out of the agency she was committed to leaving in three days' time. Better that way. She would go home now, and after lunch she would write to her principal here, who was on holiday in Yugoslavia this week.

She wouldn't tell them back home she was coming and they'd get a lovely surprise. Though her real reason was that she had a strong suspicion that if they heard Murdoch was here, they'd cable her to stay. She wasn't sure how much they would know of his movements, because they'd thought he was in Canada still, when he must have been in London, but his father and mother lived in Dunedin now and his mother had never given up hopes of a reconciliation, she was sure. Hetty Gunn and Elisabeth Keith had always been close friends. So she would go unannounced.

She would tell Tante Evelina and Uncle Ernst, but would swear them to secrecy, saying she wouldn't tell Murdoch till the eve of her departure, making it an excuse that she didn't want him to let it out to his mother, and so spoil her surprise.

Meanwhile, she must not feel as if once again her life was being cut into two halves. She must fix her mind on how wonderful it would be to walk in on Trudi, her parents, the boys, Brenda. And not, she repeated to herself, *not* on the wrench of leaving Salzburg, a Salzburg doubly dear now because Murdo was here. Oh, damn, damn, don't even think it, Theresa, you double-dyed idiot!

Think instead of darling Trudi, planning to leave Cloudy Hill because she dreaded Elisabeth having to nurse her in her old age. Theresa got up from her pocket-sized desk in the tiny room, pushed the windows wider, propped them open, gazed out over the city she loved.

She took down a scrapbook. It was the very first she had ever compiled. She sat down at the table by the window and began leafing through it. Ah, here it was. If ever a poem described what Trudi felt about

41

hills, this did. It had been written by a Tasmanian poet, Norma L. Davis, but it expressed Trudi's and Theresa's feelings exactly:

HILL-BORN
"I think that half my heart would die
If I were banished to some place
Where lowlands run to meet the sky,
And not one hill lifts up its face.

I could not bear to raise a blind
Or throw a shining window wide,
Unless my longing eyes could find
The magic of a green hillside.

I could not watch the red sun set
Across the far unbroken plain
For fear my captive heart should fret
And clamour to be home again!"

Outside her window a delivery truck was backing up the steep, cobbled street, inch by painful inch, so she did not hear the door open, or Murdoch come across the carpet. The truck stopped its manoeuvring and his shadow fell across the page. She looked up with unguarded eyes.

The next instant it was as if a shutter had dropped over them. Her lids went down and when she lifted them again the look was gone.

"I hope I didn't startle you," Murdoch said formally. "I did call out could I come in, but you couldn't hear above that noise." His eyes dropped to her book. "Oh, did you bring your scrapbooks with you?"

She nodded. "Yes, they're part of me. Part of the Theresa-who-used-to-be, young, vulnerable, often foolish. It's good to be reminded of such things. It stops me from becoming too schoolmarmish. It's an excellent thing to remember, when you're dealing with teenagers from your own age of twenty-five, how appallingly gauche you used to be, how mercurial, how plain silly!"

She looked up at him. From this angle, the over-hanging brows didn't conceal his expression so much. He looked very much like the Murdo of yesteryear, candid, open. He said, "I don't remember any gauche-ness. I do remember a gracefulness. Mercurial, yes. But then I liked you that way. Plain silly? Oh, often, but who isn't at that stage?"

Madly, she longed for him to go on. Sensibly, he didn't. He reverted to her own philosophy. "It *is* a good thing to be able to remember those things . . . how sensitive the young can be, the dread of derisive laughter, of revealing one's feelings, the crazy desire to be one of the herd, never different." He grinned and his brown face creased. "It's also a great disad-vantage at times. Many's the time my just anger has evaporated when a boy has trotted out some dilly excuse I could remember using myself, of having one of them absolutely adamant not to confess some fellow evildoer's name, and I'd recall doing the very same thing. And I'd feel, not very wisely possibly, that there might be some very good reason, or what seemed a good reason — to a child — even if to an adult absolute candour would be the best policy."

Theresa said impulsively, "But oh, what a head-master that will make you some day. A rector like your father, in a few years' time."

His eyes flickered oddly and he looked away. Then he said, "Well, at the moment I'm enjoying being a free-lance. After so many years devoted to teaching, it's a grand change to be footloose. And you — you've had your fling. You've seen the Old World, and, judging by that poem, you're thinking of going home. Ironic, isn't it?"

Her voice was crisp, her eyes, had she known, had green lights in the brown, something that always hap-pened when she was stirred. "Why ironic? I've had my two years. Maybe I've got the travel itch out of my system. It didn't have to coincide with yours."

His voice was extremely prosaic. "But it could have been very nice. We could have seen a bit of Europe and Britain together, made up our differences — just as Rudi and Lisa did — and gone home to settle down."

"Why?" She snapped it out. "Just give me one reason why! I told you my real reason for breaking it off. I feel exactly now as I did then. Did you expect long-ago airy-fairy feelings to return the moment I saw you?"

He waved a nonchalant hand. "Hardly. We're both of us older, not so likely to go into transports. But we still like the same things. Isn't being kindred spirits supposed to be a better basis than a flash-in-the-pan infatuation? Most people settle down sooner or later. I thought you might have come to your senses by now."

Theresa looked down and saw with horror that her hand had begun to clench and forced it to relax. She hoped he hadn't seen it. She would meet casualness with casualness. She shrugged, laughed.

"You've certainly lost your touch, Murdoch. When you were younger you were — were fluent. You knew the power of words. Words that could charm a woman. What you've just said would strip all romance away. Good job it doesn't matter to *me*. But in case you propose to anyone else while you're in Europe — or indeed at any time — I'd advise you not to be quite so prosaic."

"Oh, thanks. Kind of you. But I'd know exactly what *another* woman would expect."

Theresa was betrayed into natural reaction. "I bet you would," she heard herself say.

"Don't interrupt. I was going on to say I think every woman has a right to an avowal of love. You had all that . . . *once*, Tess, in the most romantic setting I could find. I'm not going to say it again — there *are* limits. But—" He put his hand into his pocket and brought something out, laid it upon the open scrapbook right in the centre of that poem.

44

An emerald ring, large, square-cut, heavy. It wobbled a little before Theresa's fascinated gaze, then settled, the light catching it from the open window and making it seem to glare balefully at her like the eye of a jungle cat. But an emerald was supposed to be the jewel of true love.

She felt as if all the breath had gone from her body, restricting her heart. She made herself relax a little, breathe in not too noticeably, then she put her hand out, picked it up, held it out to him. His eyes held hers before he took it. "Thanks all the same," she said idiotically, "but no."

"Right." He could scarcely have been more laconic. Two years had certainly changed him. He'd been a great talker. His diction, his reasoning, and a certain poetic eloquence had always fascinated Theresa. Just as well he was changed. His old persuasive powers might have made all that had happened seem unimportant. Might have made that moment of disillusionment in the early morning in Ludwigtown when she had seen him come out of Anita's cottage seem something that belonged to yesterday and wouldn't matter tomorrow and every other following day.

Theresa said, "Well, if you brought that ring, you must have had this in mind, so now you've got it off your chest, we can act normally again. There weren't any pieces to pick up, you know, no wounds for me to lick, as I told you yesterday. Perhaps your desire to comfort me was a hangover from your younger days. You always liked to play knight-errant, didn't you? Maybe you thought it would save my face. Do you know what, Murdoch Gunn? I don't give a cent if people do think Rudolf jilted me. People love to conjecture. So let 'em! I chuckle up my sleeve. But even knight-errantry seems an odd reason for a tepid sort of proposal like that. Or had you any other reason?"

"I don't think it matters if I had, or hadn't. You can probably impute half a dozen to me. You might even think, later on, pondering it, that I'm getting to

45

the stage where there just might be a headmastership offered me when I return, and you'll probably make up your mind I only asked you because it's infinitely better to be a married man in that position."

Her voice was smooth, creamy. "But why pick on me? You've always got on well with women, Murdoch. There were two or three who showed the green-eyed monster when we became engaged."

His chuckle sounded the most natural thing. "M'mm, perhaps so. But don't forget I'm well over thirty now, and most of the women of my age are already married. I wasted a lot of time waiting for you to finish your Varsity course, just being a good friend. Then your year at teachers' college, and the experience in teaching I thought you needed to satisfy you, free of domestic — and maternal — duties. I waited all that time before I even asked you, so I missed out on a few others."

"What a decidedly caddish thing to say! As if I owed you something. Like providing you with a rector's wife because you bided your time."

"Oh, it might be caddish. I don't care. We know each other well enough for plain speaking."

"I don't intend to feel remorseful. I'd have done you a great deal more harm had I not had the courage to admit to you that I'd made a mistake."

"Possibly, in fact on the face of it, yes. But it *wouldn't* have been a mistake, that I do know."

Theresa stood up, all nonchalance gone, her eyes flashing green sparks. "You insufferable prig! Sir Omnipotence! It might not have been a mistake for you, but it would have been for me. I realise this moment more than ever that I did a really wise thing when I broke our engagement. Now go—"

At that moment they heard Tante Evelina's voice from the bottom of the spindled wooden staircase. "I have made some tea, lovely tea, from the packet Murdoch brought. And there is a very nice fresh strudel. Come you down and have it."

The tension was broken. Bickering would always

die a natural death in Evelina's presence. She radiated goodness and well-being — and would be most distressed to know the walls of her house could harbour anything that savoured of discord. They looked at each other like ashamed children and descended the stairs, laughing. But Theresa found her knees were shaky.

The whole atmosphere was so disarming. Anton and his bride, Barbara, dropped in to have the evening meal with them, delighted to meet someone else from New Zealand, and Uncle Ernst sat in his usual corner, carving away at a piece of wood with the fingers of an artist.

Presently Barbara, as if sensing her mood, went across to the old beautifully and lovingly polished piano and began to play softly, and outside the soft noises of a Salzburg evening filtered in through the small open casements, girls' light laughter, men's answering deeper tones, and, coming across the river, from the festival, faint and faraway, other music.

Tante Evelina said, "Theresa told us when first she came here, Murdoch, that you had a wonderful touch with the piano. Also that you could sing the songs of your own land as musically as any Maori, and that, she said, was the highest praise possible."

Murdoch laughed. "She exaggerates. Dad was in a school in the Waikato in the North Island when I was very young, where most of the pupils were Maori, so I was in their choir. But for all that, I don't quite get that Maori energy and intonation that has a charm all their own. But I'll give it a go."

He sat down and as his fingers swept the keys, Theresa knew a great *haraeth* for the days of yesteryear. When Murdoch would sing her his Maori songs. . . .

It was a pleasant, relaxing family evening. When out in the now almost deserted street by the shop, the goodbyes to Anton and Barbara were said, Tante Evelina and Uncle Ernst said goodnight to Murdoch whose room was on the first floor, Theresa was quick to come inside. The two older people began to ascend the narrower stairs to the attic floor where they and Theresa slept.

Theresa was settling Nikolaus, the big black and white cat, in his basket again after his final outing in the garden. She came out to the tiny hall and had her foot on the first stair when Murdoch's door opened. He stood in the doorway, looking at her in the dim light of the tiny wall-lamp. In its pallor he looked a little older, tired. "Tess?" he said, "Tess . . .?"

She looked back over her shoulder at him, the thick honey-coloured hair with only a faint swirl in it swinging away from her ears. He stood there, tall, with immense shoulders, waiting, willing her to take her foot away, to come to him. And Theresa dared not.

She said lightly, "See you in the morning, Murdoch. I want to catch Tante Evelina before she goes to bed. There's something I forgot to tell her."

But she went straight to her room, shut the door, and for once turned the key as if locking herself in from the temptation to go to him, put her hands out, be received, and to the devil with pride and the memory of that long-ago betrayal.

It was the way he said her name. He had said it the way he had said it years ago. Or was she just imagining that? Theresa went across to her bookshelf and took down a much newer scrapbook, the one she had only started when she came to Salzburg. In it were the poems she had written to ease the ache in her heart, the intolerable longing. Even though she knew all the time that it was impossible for her, Theresa Keith, to marry where she did not trust.

But after she had written this one, she didn't write any more sad songs. She'd got it out of her system by writing it and after that had concentrated on poems about the Austrian countryside she so loved and had found a compensatory pleasure in having them published in German magazines. But this, of course, was written in English. It was called *The Secret*.

I loved the way you said my name those many years
        ago . . .
Through all the dreams not meant to be, it said, "I
        love you so."
    So small a thing, so sweet a thing
    To make a heart with rapture sing . . .
I loved the way you said my name those many years
        ago.
    Through all the laughter, gladness, tears,
    Of those succeeding, robber years,
    It still remains my heart's delight,
    My sun by day, my moon by night;
    The comfort of my sleepless hours,
    The scent of dead, remembered flowers . . .
    Oh, yes, a foolish little thing
    To make a heart, recalling, sing . . .
    And yet I know, I know,
    I *know*
No one has ever said my name as *you* did, long ago!

It was too hot to sleep. That was all it was . . .
just the heat. She lay without even a sheet to cover
her, but it was dawn before she fell into a doze, conscious before she did that she mustn't sleep in. She
must tell Tante Evelina early that she was going back
home because her grandmamma was relinquishing her
hold on life and Theresa could keep her in her own
home till the end, where the trees her Emil had planted
for her would nod in at the windows, where her hills
lifted up their faces, where her captive heart would
not fret and clamour to be home again.

Tante Evelina was sweet and said it was right and
proper that Maria Theresa should go home when Trudi
needed her.

It was odd, but Tante Evelina didn't seem to be
as surprised as Theresa had expected. But that was
absurd. Unless — and it was not a welcome thought,
but Tante was shrewd — unless she had a pretty good

idea that Theresa was not only responding to the call of duty, but running away from Murdoch Gunn!

She said now, hoping it sounded genuine, "I am wanting to surprise them, Tante, so I do not wish Murdoch to write to say I am coming home, so I won't tell him yet. If I leave it as long as possible, then I'd arrive at the same time as his letter, if he decided to do it."

The blue eyes were kind beneath the coronet of braided hair that was still wheat-gold. "Could you not just ask him to keep it a secret, *Liebling?* Surely the kind Murdoch would not spoil your surprise?"

"He has spoiled things for me before this, Tante. I'd rather not risk it. They're trying to book me through Pan-Am from Heathrow. I can get from Munich to London early in the morning. I can have just a few hours in Los Angeles and an hour in Tahiti, and then home. Incredible, isn't it?"

But after all, he was told that very day because while they were washing the breakfast dishes, the agency rang to say that due to a cancellation, she could be on her way a day or two sooner than planned. Failing that, it might be three or four. Theresa said, "Then I'll take the cancellation," and turned from the telephone to meet Murdoch's eyes.

"I'll be getting off home the day after tomorrow, Murdoch. I want to give them a surprise, so don't tell anyone by letter till I've managed to get there, will you? It's the only thing to do, I can live at Cloudy Hill and Trudi will be able to stay there till — as long as she needs to."

"Fair enough," he said, and turned to Tante Evelina. "Is there a dry cloth? Theresa always did use too much detergent in the water and it soaks the towels." Theresa felt as if someone had used a candle-snuffer on her.

CHAPTER THREE

TANTE EVELINA went into instant action. Theresa must not wear herself out rushing round to say good-bye to everyone. There must be a little party, a little ingathering. That would be tomorrow night. They would make it an early one, commencing at six, then everyone would go home at an early hour, so Theresa would have a reasonable night's sleep, before her world trip. Tante Evelina clucked her tongue. "It is bad enough to travel across the world from England, but to go right from München, even more foolish, and in such exhausting, hot weather too. But then the young are like that. Though in turn, as your own children grow up, you will croak just like us old ones. Rudolf and Lisa will take you to München, however, and no doubt Murdoch will accompany them."

Murdoch heard this as he came into the room and said, "I'm sorry, but I won't be able to. I'm booked with that crowd at the pension to go to Berchtes-gaden that day. They're going to Obersalzberg too, and down the salt-mines. I can't cancel because to make it worth while they had to have a certain num-ber and roped me in."

Theresa curled her lip, her back to him. He wouldn't have taken much persuasion. She could just imagine that lovely girl who'd loaned her the swim-suit clutch-ing Murdoch tightly round the waist as they went down the chutes into the mines. At that moment, con-firming this, the telephone rang. A pleasant, unmis-takably Canadian voice asked for Murdoch. It was quite a long conversation.

Theresa had her case in the sitting-room, quite near, and could hear bits of it. She heard him say, "A very good idea. You'd get a refund on the return half of your tour. And why not take a teaching position here when you like it so much? Far too many people take all their working holidays in Britain, and see very little of the Continent. You could even make your way to New Zealand in stages, you know. Live for a while in Italy, in Greece. Perhaps join up with one of those overland parties, going through India and so on, if you really want to see the world, and then fly to New Zealand from Singapore."

She passed Murdoch as he was putting the phone down. He said, "By the way, keep tonight free. I've got tickets for chamber music in the Schloss Mirabell." Just like that!

Theresa said quickly, "That was a bit of a risk. I'm sorry, but I must go across to Aigen tonight to see a friend of mine. I just can't go away without a farewell visit to her and she can't come tomorrow night, Tante said." She added, "But perhaps you could ask that nice Canadian girl."

"The whole crowd are going to the Festival. It was booked before they left Canada. I'll—" but the phone cut him off.

He answered it, speaking slowly in German. It was evident the caller at the other end knew who he was, and chatted on. Suddenly Theresa had her suspicions when he said, "Oh, I can assure you Theresa will be delighted. It will fit in beautifully with her plans. I'm so delighted you can make the party."

Theresa stared at his back with unbelief. No, it couldn't be! It was. He finished up with *"Auf Wiedersehn,* Maria." He turned, grinning. "We go to the chamber music. Maria informs me that her sister is able, after all, to babysit for Johann and Alois. Now take that look off your face. This way we catch up on something we'd always planned to do . . . have an evening of chamber music in Salzburg."

(*That* had been in the days when they had planned a honeymoon here. *That* had been vastly different, but she wouldn't let him see how much she minded.)

So she said mildly, "Oh, I just thought how autocratic you are. That's why I looked like that. I'll enjoy the music, of course, but it's a pity you're so set on having your own way. Most men would have understood that I could have a hundred things to do tonight."

"I do understand it. I also know that with your passion for music, you'd rather by far work into the early hours packing than forgo a farewell visit there. You'll be thirteen thousand miles away from such things soon."

By the evening she had lost her irritation with him. It would be a night to remember. Not as they had planned it long ago, but nevertheless, something shared. Music could transport them both into a world where discord simply could not exist.

Theresa wore a long cotton evening dress with an Empire bodice, tied at its high waistline with green velvet ribbon. It was green patterned on white, and its hem was a deep green flounce. It was simple and effective and brought up the glints of green in the hazel-brown eyes. Her hair shone like a pale candle above it and she wore a pendant that had been a gift to Trudi from her first young husband who had been killed in that long-ago war, an emerald surrounded by tiny white diamonds — once Theresa had worn a ring that had been bought to match it, on her left hand. . . .

They came into the intricately ornate building, with its air of another world. Murdoch said, "I feel we men ought to be wearing knee-breeches and have powdered hair and silver buckles on our shoes. You women fare better. Present-day evening dress for women fits in beautifully. Frills and embroidery — and that high waistline." His eyes met hers. Susceptible Murdo, thought Theresa, hardening her heart against him.

Yet surely here was the setting for high romance . . . this place that had known centuries of intrigue and scandal and rich living, fashioned by craftsmen with art in their fingertips, enhanced by priceless treasures in its day, peopled now by those who had come with warm expectancy in their hearts, knowing they were to be caught up by the strains of incomparable music into the magic of another day and age.

It wasn't a large room, but the seating capacity was taxed to the full. The murmuring died away as two young musicians took their places on the dias, one at the beautiful piano, one with a violin. They had slender figures and Byronic hair-styles, and suddenly Murdoch and Theresa were transported into another world. A world of dreams.

Brahms . . . Dvorak . . . and, of course, Mozart. All enmity died between them, unable to exist in the presence of harmonies like these. Theresa was aware of almost intolerable longing.

They came out into the balminess of the Salzburg night. There above them was the fortress, haloed in the luminosity of its floodlighting against that blue velvet sky. A little cloud floated lovingly over it. The stars glowed.

"You must come here by daylight, Murdoch, when you're living here, and film that. It's one of the most perfectly photogenic scenes in all Europe."

"It gives one the most incredible feeling to stand in rooms where they wrote their poetry, their music, painted their pictures or wrought their poems in stone out of rough blocks from the hillsides. To finger a desk where treaties were signed, or the documents of surrender, to imagine the kings and emperors and dictators of the past dining in sumptuous halls and perhaps never knowing — quite — the peace of mind we know. I felt this very strongly when I stood upon the Heights of Abraham and thought of Wolfe and Montcalm. That once it was spoiled by the hideousness of war."

Theresa thudded back to earth. Canada! And the Canadian girl Theresa had liked so much that night at the Doktorwirt — against her will. She was such a kindred spirit, so friendly and wholesome. So if Theresa found her kindred, wouldn't Murdoch? She too was an outdoor girl, taught history, English, French. Catriona McCorkill. Weren't the McCorkills kin to the Gunns? They even wore the Gunn tartan.

Oh, yes, Murdoch and Catriona could — would find a lot in common.

It was out before she knew it. "Had you met Catriona before you came here, Murdoch?" She felt instantly dismayed and added rather lamely, "Mentioning the Heights of Abraham made me think of it. Catriona mentioned them too, when she joined us for coffee after the swim."

He was very frank. "Yes, of course. She's got relations in New Zealand, in Oamaru. In fact a cousin of hers was on the staff at Waitaki. I met him at a teachers' meeting and she asked me to look them up. Her people were extremely kind to me, showed me places in Montreal and Quebec I'd never have known about otherwise. And a dozen other places too. Fascinating. That's why I was so sure I could borrow bathing-suits for you and Lisa from her and her friend."

Theresa had to ask it. "Was it just coincidence you met up with her here?"

"Good lord, no. I was all set to stay longer in London. But when Catriona wrote she was coming to Europe for this holiday tour, I changed my plans. Good job I did, or I wouldn't have seen you."

Her voice was dry with derision. "Yes, good thing, or everyone back home would be saying, 'How too cruel . . . what a pity they missed each other.' Now they can think we met, but weren't interested in making it up." Then something hit her right between the eyes and once more she came out with it before she could have second thoughts. "Then what *was* all that twaddle about bringing the ring over and asking me — asking me — to wear it again? You take awful risks — that *could* have gone to my head, Murdoch. The thought of you setting off with it in your pocket and trying your luck again!"

There was the suggestion of a pause, then the hint of a drawl in his voice as they walked on. "Well, it didn't come off, did it? I'm caught out. How would you feel if I came clean and simply told you I couldn't face local jewellers with it, and, having heard you get very good prices in London, brought it with me?"

She had to lie to save her pride because she felt — how did she feel? Devastated? No, more like desolate. She managed presently to say with what she hoped was a convincing pretence, "I'd feel much better, Murdoch. If a girl consents to become engaged to a chap, then finds she doesn't love him enough to spend the rest of her life with him, she does have him on her conscience rather. Feels guilty. It worried me when you produced that ring. I'd like to think you made up your mind this parting is for good and reshape your life just as I've re-shaped mine." Then something else hit her. "What *did* make you ask me again, if you hadn't intended to when you left?"

His voice was hard. "Couldn't it just have been that you bowled me over again?"

"No. You wouldn't have made it a prosaic proposition like that if it had happened that way."

Now his voice was slow and deliberate. "Perhaps you came pretty near the truth yesterday. There's a headmastership I've always coveted. It could be coming up fairly soon. Since leaving Canada I've reason to believe it could be offered to me if I applied, certainly that I'd be on the short list for it. It's time I settled down. I've been told they would much prefer a married man, so—"

Theresa said furiously, "Thank you *very* much. That's all it needed. I've no doubt you'll find yourself a life partner to suit your requirements, Murdoch, but let me give you one word of advice. Don't tell her *why* you want to marry her — you might get your face slapped." She could have slapped it there and then when he laughed. "Let her at least keep *some* illusions. Let her think it's for love. And don't make it Catriona."

"Why not, for heaven's sake?"

"Because she's too nice for you, that's why. Now listen, Murdoch. This is my last night but one in Salzburg. I may never be here again, and I've loved

56

it so. Let's walk the rest of the way in silence. I want to savour every moment, not feel rubbed up the wrong way."

After a little while the too-rapid beating of Theresa's heart subsided and she tried to tell herself this was the way she wanted it . . . quietness in which to absorb the little sounds of this loved city, the footsteps echoing on the pavements, the soft lap-lap of the Salzach against its banks, the sighing and rustling of the trees.

They came up the steepness of the street and Murdoch unlocked the side door beside the shop and let them into the tiny entrance from which the stairs to the living quarters rose up steeply.

He caught her to him, taking her unawares. She brought her hands up smartly, clutched him by each arm, tried to push him away. Her voice, pitched low not to disturb the others in the house, was furious.

"Murdo! No — it's ridiculous when we've just—" but the rest of the hot words were lost under his kiss.

Shame flooded over her that she should still feel like this, as if her very spirit blended with his beneath the touch of his mouth. She could feel herself yielding . . . or wanting to yield. She had just enough strength left in her to — the next moment — go rigid, tighten her mouth against his. Nevertheless, it lasted quite a while.

Then he lifted his head, laughed, said, "I've never kissed a woman against her will before. Quite an experience. It's got something."

When he laughed, she had to clench her fists so she didn't yield to the temptation to strike him. He said, "Oh, come, Theresa, you aren't just a child now. Don't be so naïve. Put it down to experience. I think you're too idealistic. I knew when we became engaged that I was the only man you'd ever kissed. I liked it then. But be your age. All kisses aren't betrothal ones, or binding in any way. Pity you take yourself so seriously."

The next moment she wasn't there to answer him

back. She'd picked up her skirts and gone running up the stairs, and she didn't stop till she'd reached the haven of her own room.

She gazed helplessly round the room, unable to concentrate. She ought to go on with some packing. People would be coming in and out all day tomorrow. An hour now would accomplish much. But she couldn't. She flung her clothes off and got into bed, childishly wishing it were cooler, so that she could have pulled the clothes right over her head. Surprisingly enough she fell into a deep, exhausted sleep from which Tante Evelina roused her all too soon, with a cup of coffee.

Tante said smilingly, "I knew you'd want to be up early, *Liebling,* because it was not likely you would have wanted to go on with the mundane task of packing last night when you had had a romantic evening of moonlight and music."

Romantic fiddlesticks, thought Theresa. Tante sat down on the bed, her eyes kind, and Theresa shrank inwardly. Was she going to give her some advice, matchmaking-wise?

But Tante said placidly, "I think it is wise you should go, Maria Theresa, though it will leave a big gap in this house. But we knew we could not have you for ever."

Theresa said quickly, because she was blinking tears away, "But it's not as much of a wrench as once it was, even if New Zealand really is at the other side of the world. Now travel is so quick and air fares greatly reduced, it seems nearer. When Trudi married my grandfather, she knew she might never see Austria again. And she never has. At first, of course, there wasn't the money. Then when she and Granddad were planning a visit, he died so suddenly."

Tante nodded. "But when you get home, child, it will infuse new life into her. You will show her your coloured photos, your slides, you will talk with her more fluently in German than you used to do, and you have a gift of words, because you write poetry, and it shows in your speech, and it will come alive again for her. And don't forget, of course, that she knew greatest happiness of all in New Zealand. And tell her that next year we will hope to spend Weihnachten with her." Tante's eyes twinkled. "Trudi will forget all about going into a Home and will start planning what to cook for us for the Christmas after next, you will see!"

The hours sped. Theresa finished her packing quickly, leaving Uncle Ernst to despatch the rest. People who couldn't come to the ingathering dropped in to say goodbye, the telephone rang incessantly, and she was thankful, for she was never alone with Murdoch and had managed to greet him quite naturally, though not warmly, that morning at breakfast.

Tante Evelina decreed the party must not go on too late, as so much travelling was ahead of Theresa, so all the gaiety and farewelling were telescoped into a very few hours.

The moment for saying goodbye to Murdoch came even before she had to say goodbye to her uncle and aunt. "What a very early start for the salt-mines," Tante Evelina had remarked just before the party started and Murdoch had told her he must be up by six the next morning.

After breakfast Murdoch said he would walk down into the town to pick up the car. They all trooped downstairs to say goodbye to him. Theresa told herself that if he gave her a light kiss on the cheek she wasn't to flinch. But he didn't. He just said, "Well, cheerio, Tess. Give my love to everyone at Ludwigtown, especially Trudi. And if Mum and Dad come up to their cottage at Labour Weekend, the same to them. Hope you have a smooth trip over. So-long."

So-long. Such a funny little farewell word, usually said as a nonchalant sort of goodbye, meaning they'd meet again soon. But perhaps it had a pathos all its own, because it *would* be so long before she saw him again. Unless he got this New Zealand job. But it could be far enough away. After all, New Zealand was bigger than Britain and divided into two islands at that.

She matched his casualness with her own. "Bye-bye. Have a good time here," and then as he took two steps away, words involuntarily sprang to her lips. "Murdoch, be careful driving. You aren't used to the right side of the road."

She could have bitten her tongue out next moment. He turned round, grinned, said, "Yes, Grandmam-ma," and went off down the cobbled hill, grinning.

Tante Evelina's eyes were wise and kind and Theresa had to avoid them.

Things became less tense once the goodbyes to her uncle and aunt had been made and she was off with Rudolf and Lisa, because they were young and much-travelled, and she would see them every snow-sports season in New Zealand. To them the world didn't seem half so large. To people who travelled to the Antipodes in ships, taking a month or five weeks, it was a long voyage. But in today's jumbo jets non-sense was made of thirteen thousand miles.

In no time she was at Heathrow and had just a short time before her plane left for Los Angeles at one p.m. It was Friday and by British time she would be touching down at Auckland by seven-thirty Satur-day night, though, as they would cross the date-line somewhere in the Pacific, it would be seven-thirty Sun-day morning in New Zealand. How incredible to be riding time out and skipping a whole night!

Nevertheless, she became very conscious she was doing just that as they zoomed on. Because although they flew into the sunset, it retreated before them, as if time itself was slipping back from the edge of twilight into bright mid-afternoon again. To Theresa it was as magical as a trip to the moon. . . .

Once the Pacific was below her Theresa knew she was really going home. This sea washed the shores of her own land, twelve flying hours away. It was rather frustrating to have just one hour in Tahiti, but the private conversations of the airport employees in French made her feel she was back in Europe again. It made her dizzy trying to work out what time it would be in Salzburg, in London, in Los Angeles, in New Zealand.

Theresa walked up and down the lounge and out on the terrace, drinking in the savours of the tropics, the spiciness of the atmosphere, watching dim outlines of mountains and hills, the light shining on hibiscus blooms near at hand.

The soft Tahitian-French voices made her realise that some day, if she had itchy feet, she need not go as far as Europe. She could take a cruise to Tahiti and New Caledonia, and practise her French. Sometimes from New Zealand parties of high school students took holidays here. She might organise one. Oh, yes, there were more things in life than getting married. There could be shorter, cheaper trips, to Australia, so vast that one would need half a dozen vacations to explore it, to Fiji, Samoa, the Cook Islands. Ah, it was time to board the plane again.

Theresa, worn out by all the experiences of the last week, slept like a babe till she was wakened by the steaming hot towels provided for freshening up, prior to breakfast.

Now the sun was coming up. Oh, what a privilege to see, at this height, the dawn painting the clouds with rose and amethyst, and fire of gold, and touching the azure of the sky with iridescent glints till its inverted bowl looked like the inside of a giant *paua* shell, glittering with rainbow colours.

Someone said, "There she is!" Beneath them was the curving beauty of the twin harbours of Auckland, the Manukau and the Waitemata, which was living up to its name and looking as smooth as the surface of obsidian. In the centre of it, moulded by volcanic action into symmetrical loveliness was the island of Rangitoto. And the city itself, centred with high-rise buildings, had spread into dozens of bush-clad bays and inlets, in marine suburbs, and was linked with the North Shore residential areas by a shining slenderly built harbour bridge, a city that housed nearly half a million people.

How heart-warming to be back in the brightness of this semi-tropical city, even though it was an early spring day, and to hear New Zealand voices, though in an international airport, other languages always interspersed. Maoris and Islanders mingled in the throng, a good mixture, she thought, her senses sharpened by so long away from it. She got through Customs, picked up her flight ticket at the N.A.C. counter, had some coffee.

Her plane would stop at Wellington but was bypassing Christchurch, so she would be in Dunedin by early afternoon, in time to get the Mount Cook plane to Queenstown.

Things went very smoothly. A very wonderful way to travel to your own part of the globe on a day as crystal-clear as this, sharp as an etching because there were no heat hazes or smog dullings.

Soon they were airborne again, heading out across Cook Strait to the mountains of the South Island and the East Coast. When, an hour or two later, Theresa could look down and see the long arms of the sheltering peninsula hills reaching out to embrace Otago Harbour, and the steepled city of Dunedin scattered on its hills, she knew a quickening of the heart. Here she had attended university, here Murdoch had taught during his long patient courtship, if it could have been called that. She'd had a struggle not to be jealous of the older staff members of his school, girls who were just that much nearer his age, possibly more satisfying for him.

It had been a minor wonder when, quite suddenly, in the April of her second year of teaching at the school in Ludwigtown, Murdoch had proposed. Had told her that all those years he had just bided his time. And she had believed him. Oh, what a sucker! All the time there must have been other women, especially one, an older, more fascinating, more experienced woman.

Theresa saw the Maungatuas across the Taieri Plain, the dear simplicity of Momona Airport, circled by fields, and shut her mind to all looking back. There was the little plane that would take her home. There wasn't much time for boarding it. People were going out to it now. She made it. How strange to rise up in such a midget after the jumbo jets, but how wonderful to head west, to see the blue-green ribbon of the huge Clutha river snaking through gorges and hills that even in spring, after the richly fertilised hills of Austria, looked a little parched. But the valleys showed great emerald patches.

Then, what she looked for most of all, the Remarkables, that range of mountains that had been her view from her bedroom window as long as she could remember. Yes, there they were, as jagged as ever, saw-toothed and wicked-looking, sticking up into the sky much the way the Dolomites did, when you crossed the border from Austria into Italy. Lake Wakatipu lay in deep blueness, a long dog-leg-shaped lake over fifty miles long, Bayonet Peaks sticking up over the waters, Cecil Peak, Walter Peak, further down was the Humboldt Range, and the long arm of Ben Lomond. They swept down the lake, so she had the lovely view of Queenstown with the Skyline Gondolas ascending, bright bubbles against the dark serrated pines, then they circled, zoomed back, came to land at the eastern end. Frankton Airport . . . home!

It had to be, of course, in a tiny place like this — someone who knew her, Ngaio Lawrie, meeting a friend. Her voice squeaked with surprise. "Theresa . . . why, I was speaking to your mother this morning at church and she never said you were coming home."

Theresa laughed. "She didn't know. I'm in the nature of a surprise. I just decided to pack up my traps and come home. It's so easy now. Just imagine, I left Austria Friday morning, and here I am, Sunday afternoon. As good a time as any to walk in on them.

I expect they'll all be home today, if not at the Ridge, at Cloudy Hill, seeing Trudi's not been too well. In fact that's what decided me to come home. If Trudi's past her work and talking of going into a Home in Invercargill, it's time I was back. I'll live with her. I expect Dad or one of the boys would stay with her if Mother went to church this morning."

Ngaio looked a little confused. "I thought they were all there. Is Trudi really not well? I mean, past her work doesn't sound like her. In fact, at the Institute Luncheon last week I was eating apfelstrudel under the distinct impression it was hers."

"It must have been Mother's. Does seem incredible, doesn't it? Trudi's always been more energetic than anyone, bustling round, filling her days to the brim. But perhaps you've not seen her for some time."

Ngaio said, "Oh, but I — no, I expect it was longer than I thought. And old people, even ones like Trudi, can suddenly go downhill. Look, I'm in no hurry. My friend would like a slightly longer drive, I'm sure. I'll drop you over at Ludwigtown before going round to Speargrass Flat. It would save you ringing your people to come and get you. It would be more of a surprise if you can just walk in on them. If you'd just wait a moment, I've got to phone someone."

"Right. I'd thought of trying to get a taxi, but they've all gone and I'd have to wait. I'd planned to walk in unannounced."

Theresa looked about her with greedy eyes all the way home, hoping things she'd loved before she went away hadn't been changed out of all recognition. She marvelled that she'd ever found the courage to leave it. The poplars at Windy Corner had grown much taller, there was more ivy and virginia creeper on the old stone fences the pioneers had patiently built as they removed the glacial stones from their pastures; there was a new long-needed bridge over Goldpan Creek, the walk along the banks of the Awhitu River had been lengthened by nearly half a mile and young blossom trees planted, and Gabriel Longshanks had actually painted his roof. It had been red with rust when she'd gone away.

Ngaio laughed, said, "Gabriel is married, no less, and a reformed character. He shaves every day now, keeps the hens in a run and wears a white shirt on a Sunday. Never seen such a change in a man."

They branched away from the Arrowtown Road and turned right towards the Crown Range where the Awhitu River snaked out from its dark gorge once so fabulously rich in gold, and spread out to water the rich river terraces above the more powerful Kawarau before it joined it to hurtle eastwards to the Pacific. Here lay the prosperous farmlands that clustered about Ludwigtown.

Ngaio took a side-road and turned up a lane leading off it; Theresa saw the white gleaming boards of her father's house, built just thirty years ago, the green tiles, the big woolshed and the open doors of the enormous treble-sized garage.

"Not even the truck's there," she said, "they must all be over at Trudi's. Oh dear, I hope nothing necessitates them all being there. I'd have thought the boys would have been home."

Ngaio went past the gate and up a smaller lane sweet with hawthorn not yet in bloom, but thick with foliage and buds, daffodils ribboning the edge beneath, and in over cattle-stops to halt beside an old summerhouse that, but for the clematis and wistaria binding its latticed walls, would have fallen down.

The house still wasn't in sight, but Theresa had said she wanted to walk in, not have the sound of a car announce someone's arrival.

She thanked Ngaio, put her case and hand-luggage in the summerhouse, waved her goodbyes to Ngaio and her friend, carried on past the bend in the hawthorns and stopped dead, overcome with joy. There it was, Cloudy Hill!

CHAPTER FOUR

TOURISTS were sometimes seen to blink their eyes
at their first glimpse of the Cloudy Hill homestead
when one of the coach drivers decided to run them
past for the fun of it. They would wonder aloud if
they were in the Southern Hemisphere or the middle
of Europe.

It was wooden, brown, with overhanging eaves of
carved lacework above the balconies under each eave,
and window-boxes of scarlet geraniums hung there,
despite the fact that geraniums wintered very happily
outside in New Zealand, even here among the mountains. Later petunias in whites, reds and purples would
splash their colours from those same boxes, and aub-
rietias hang in blue cascades.

The roofs, on different levels, were steep, which
was a good thing here, and though no animals ever
needed to winter inside, the lower floor exactly re-
sembled the houses overseas that provided for this,
and on the stone-floored verandahs, made of glacier-
planed rocks from the hillsides, were more tubs of
geraniums and climbing plants of all varieties, so dear
to Trudi's heart. The boys weren't sitting on the
verandah benches. Theresa had a horrible feeling that
the whole house was watching and waiting. For what?
Surely they weren't all gathered about Trudi's bed-
side?

So instead of bursting in with a blithe, "Surprise,
surprise!" she came in very quietly, tiptoeing, and heard
a murmur of voices from the living-room. It had a
glass-panelled door, slightly veiled with a nylon cur-
tain, but against the light of the windows opposite,
she could see the whole scene.

It looked ordinary enough. They must have had a
late midday dinner, and were sitting round the table
still, finishing their coffee . . . Mother, Father, Josef,
Wilhelm. Not Trudi or Brenda.

Theresa pushed open the door, said in a voice that had gone dry, "Where's Trudi, where is she?"

The effect was almost electric. Four figures sprang to their feet, gaped, then surged forward, with Elisabeth Keith well in the lead. She caught her girl to her, said, "Trudi's in bed, love, but where, where on earth have you sprung from?"

Tears were spilling down Theresa's cheeks. "Not from the earth, from the sky. It was her letter — the one you finished. She was thinking of going into a Home in Invercargill — remember? She was worrying about you trying to run two households. So I came home to live with her."

"Good for you, Tess!" exulted Joe, swinging her up off her feet after he'd pushed her mother away. Bill shoved him off in turn and kissed his sister. Roderick Keith waited till they were done, rather patiently, as if he wasn't as moved as they were, but Theresa saw his jaw tighten and flung herself at him. "Oh, Dad, I can't imagine why I stayed away so long. But tell me, how is Trudi?"

"Oh, not really ill, Tess. Just tired. Resting."

"Resting! Trudi! Why, she'd have to be ill to be resting."

"Not these days. Merely lethargic, a lessening of energy. I expect it comes to us all. Tess, I'll go through and tell her you're here. It oughtn't to be too sudden."

Theresa saw Joe grin and Bill grin back. What was so funny about that?

She said, "What are you two grinning like that for? There's—"

Joe said hastily, "It's okay. Just my perverted sense of humour. It sounded as if the sight of Theresa would give anyone a shock."

"Now I know I'm home again — a truly brotherly remark! For the past two years I've been treated with the utmost courtesy. It would do you two good to go to Austria for a year or two."

She thought Joe looked relieved. But why? Oh, she must be imagining things. Joe said hurriedly, "Well,

I don't wonder if they did treat you like that, Sis. Maybe absence makes the heart grow fonder — even about a sister; I never thought I'd think my own sister dishy, but so help me, you are!"

Theresa blinked. "Heavens, my legs will hardly support me. That from you, Joe Keith, is the most surprising thing that's happened to me in all my twenty-five years. But where's Brenda?"

Bill said, "In North Otago, on a farm, *Deo gratias*."

"You horrible thing! Surely she's not as bad as that?"

"She's the bane of our existence. You've no idea what we've been through since she started High School. She's gone all analytical. It's ghastly. Joe and I are conducting our love-life in secret as far as is humanly possible.

"Really? Oh, it'll be just another of her phases. She's always been like this, one wild enthusiasm after another." Suddenly she looked horrorstricken. "I've just thought — she's in Form One. I'll bet I get landed with her for English!" She added: "I've applied from overseas for a position here. Thought I'd live here, instead of over home, then that would put an end to this nonsense about Trudi going to Invercargill. If I don't get the position I'll go waitressing."

Bill began to say something, but checked himself. Theresa said curiously, "What were you going to say, Bill?" He seemed tongue-tied then, and then she got it. "Oh, do you think Trudi needs someone with her all the time? In that case, I'll cancel my application."

His father answered for Bill, "Of course not. Your mother can keep an eye on her during the day. It would be a great relief to know you were here at night, Tessa. It's far too much for your mother — besides," he grinned, "I must admit I don't like sleeping solo."

Theresa saw the two boys exchange a look that said: Heavens . . . at his age! She wanted to laugh. She felt years older than them.

Roderick said, "Ah, here's your mother now."

Elisabeth led the way upstairs. Trudi certainly looked smaller and rather lost amid the billows of the Austrian type bed, and she hadn't much colour, but she didn't look at her last gasp. Theresa knelt by the bed, put her arms round her, and saw two big tears well up in the blue eyes and roll down the crêpey cheeks. Yes, those cheeks had been smooth and still rosy when she had gone away.

"Oh, *Liebling, Liebling*," said the old lady brokenly, "this makes my eyes glad. But you ought not to have come because of me, unless . . ."

"Unless I was 'wearying for my 'ain folk' as Granny Keith used to say. And I was, pet. I'm full of plans. I've applied for a position at the school, and it will be much better doing prep at nights and marking papers and setting tests in the quietness of Cloudy Hill than over at the Ridge. You know what Joe and Bill are, records always on, to say nothing of Brenda. The boys tell me she's rather a handful just now."

She was glad when Trudi chuckled. That was more like her.

Elisabeth said, "She fancies herself as a sort of marriage guidance counsellor just now. Advice to the love-lorn and all that. It's very trying."

Theresa said, "What on earth set her off on that?"

Elisabeth groaned. "You know she's always been a crony of Gabriel Longshanks? Well, after Humphrey Richards passed on word that he'd met the woman Gabriel had wanted as his wife long ago, old Gabriel used Brenda as a wailing wall. She tried to persuade him to write to her, but he just hadn't the nerve. She winkled the address of the guest-house she was running in Jersey out of Humphrey, and sat down and wrote to Eloise and told her every single thing Gabriel had told her and — of course — added a few frills of her own."

"Within ten days of getting Eloise's reply — not quite committing herself but very nearly — Gabriel was flying to London and on to Jersey, so smartened up — Brenda even took him shopping — that the pilot of the Mount Creek plane didn't even recognise him! We went down and had a working bee on his house, and they're blissfully happy. But the upshot of it is that that child positively smirks every time she sees them and thinks now she's God's gift to Ludwigtown in affairs of the heart.

Theresa burst out laughing, then sobered up and looked alarmed. "Well, I think I'll have second thoughts about taking the teaching job if it's offered. There are always young unmarried men on the staff and it could be very embarrassing. I'd better try for a world of my own at some tourist hotel."

Trudi said, "No, little one. Your gifts would be wasted there. I think you would get this position. I heard someone was leaving. Your facility with languages would stand you in great stead. They would know you could fill in if any of the other language teachers had to be away. And at school, even Brenda is subdued. A little First Former doesn't get much chance to — what is it? — throw her weight around."

Theresa looked sharply at her step-grandmamma. There was a flake of colour in each cheek now and a glow in the blue eyes. Their glances met — Theresa's smilingly. Trudi immediately closed her eyes and said in a fainter voice, "And now I would like to doze. Come and see me in an hour's time, *Liebling*. I will be refreshed then."

Theresa said contritely, "Oh, Mother, I've tired her. I suppose it's the excitement. I ought to have let you know."

"Yes, perhaps so, dear, but never mind, a little sleep and she'll want to see you again. Come along."

It was just as well for Theresa's peace of mind that she did not see her mother look back at the bed as she gently closed the door, or the occupant of it close one eye in a very wicked wink!

Under cover of the general chatter and washing-up, Theresa managed to tell them, without need to look at them because she was at the sink, that what did they think? — who should have turned up her last week in Salzburg but Murdoch Gunn! "He'd tagged on to some tourist party. I think he was quite keen on this teacher in it he'd met in Quebec. A gorgeous girl, Catriona McCorkill. She'd suit Murdoch beautifully. Even a clan connection there. No old feuds to disturb things."

"What rubbish you talk, Theresa," said her father, chuckling. "That wasn't what upset the apple-cart between you and Murdoch. Those things belong to the past. But he'd always been around, so I suppose he didn't seem glamorous enough. You had to fall for the unknown."

Murdoch not glamorous. Not stirring. If only they knew! Theresa wrung out the dishcloth with such fervour it split. She mopped madly at a pool on the bench. "I think the whole family had better know about that. I can't stand being made to look a starry-eyed fool. I was *never* in love with Rudolf. All he ever talked about was Lisa, from the start. They'd quarrelled. He thought a spot of jealousy might jerk her into knowing she really loved him. The first idea he had was to send a photo of us, looking sentimental. *That* gave me *my* great idea. And it worked. She did care when, at my suggestion, I accompanied him there."

Bill said incredulously, "But starve the lizards, Sis, you surely didn't dish Murdoch for a mad plan like—"

She swung round on him, aware her parents' eyes were fastened on her, "Oh, for Pete's sake, Bill, of course I didn't. I said that gave me *my* great idea. It wasn't pure altruism on my part. I wanted to give Murdoch up. I felt trapped. I'd never known anyone but him in that sort of way. I'd hero-worshipped him for years — I admit that. I was very flattered when he proposed — an older man, a great sportsman, an intellectual as well. But frankly, in the end, he bored me."

71

She thought they all stiffened a little. Oh, how tiresome this was! She said a little hotly, "Oh, I know you all think there's no one like Murdoch Gunn. But me, I've been round the world a little and I know there are better fish in the sea. Two things decided me to come home — your letter, Mum, saying Trudi was failing, and Murdoch turning up in Salzburg. My guess is that now I've turned him down again, he'll marry this Catriona McCorkill, and if he doesn't get some position here in New Zealand that he covets, he'll maybe take one in Canada. I'm here to do a job, look after Trudi. I just ask you to accept the fact, as you did when you thought I'd fallen for Rudi, that Murdoch Gunn has gone out of my life for good. Tomorrow I'll hop over and see the Rector to find out how my application fared. I put a note in with it, saying not to let me know by letter, that I'd be home very soon."

Her father said slowly, "Mr. Guthrie's still on holiday in Oamaru. He's taking things easy, had a coronary, so he might retire a bit sooner than expected. He bought a section here long ago. I expect they'll build next year and retire to it. They got one on Kingfisher Hill, said they couldn't bear to be without the view of the lake they've lived with so long."

Theresa said in utter dismay, "I only hope he doesn't retire too soon. Perhaps that's selfish, but I'd love to have a year or two under him again." She pulled a face. "Listen to me! I may not even get the position. I expect it's still being advertised."

Her father shook his head. "No. In fact, I hope you didn't miss the bus. I think we'll hear soon, one way or the other. I reckon you would have a good chance, with your improved German. Well, boys, we must get over home."

Again Theresa was aware that the boys were subduing grins. Really, they were as mad as ever. Perhaps they were at the age where they thought *they* ran the farm and Dad was practically superfluous!

Roderick said shortly as if he were aware of it, "Now off with you. Elisabeth, we'll get our own tea. Can't expect you to tear yourself away when your daughter's just got home. We'll come over for the evening. I'll want to hear about Salzburg. Hope you've got your slides with you. I'll never forget the three months we had there five years ago. Right, boys, vamoose!"

It was marvellous to be with Mother again. She and Theresa had been such pals. Theresa spilled out the contents of her case and hand-luggage all over the floor of the spare bedroom, bringing out souvenirs, photos, postcards. Time flew. Then they tiptoed along to peep at Trudi, who was just awake, she said, and refreshed. She said she couldn't bear to stay in bed and miss all the fun and there was so much she wanted to ask. So she was getting up and would be as right as a trivet, and don't keep fussing!

It sounded so much like the Trudi of old that Theresa took heart. The fire was glowing bright gold, apple-blossom tapped against the windows, daffodils encircled the orchard trees, grape-hyacinths that Mother always called matchheads ribboned the flower-beds with blue, and Trudi's geese, complete with fluffy goslings, walked proudly in pairs.

Mother had certainly lost weight, but it suited her. She was as slim as Theresa herself. Perhaps at that age, it was a bit thin, but she looked stylish. "I love that dress, Mother."

Elisabeth looked down. "Yes, I've got a coat to match. Wore it to church this morning. What a rush we had, too — had a puncture on the way. But the boys got the wheel off in a trice, and wouldn't let your father help at all."

Theresa said, "You all managed to go? Nobody stayed with Trudi?"

Trudi came in. "It was one of my better days. Martha came over, and kept an eye on the dinner too. Now you and your mother must make your bed up. Tomorrow you can get some of your things from

73

over at the new homestead. You'll want your desk and your notebooks — plenty room for them here."

Theresa laughed. "I may not need them. Mustn't count my chickens. I may be washing dishes at the pub yet, or serving in the store. May I have the bedroom next to yours?"

Trudi nodded. "That will be best. Then I shall know if I call out in the night, someone will hear and come."

How poignant it seemed to have Trudi dependent upon others. Trudi who had nursed them all, who'd run two households without sign of strain when Mother had been so ill after Brenda's birth, and Trudi had refused to let Theresa stay home from school.

She knew a full and real happiness in being home. Even if Trudi became, in time, so frail she needed someone in the house all the time, it would not worry Theresa. She had been brought up by mother and grandmother to rejoice in housekeeping. If she had married Murdoch she wouldn't have wanted to continue her academic career. Certainly she loved teaching, had never wanted to do anything else as a way of earning her living, but the most satisfying work in the world was home-making.

So much of it was sheer delight . . . the sheen on old furniture, firelight reflected in panelling, crusty loaves and scones cooling on wire grids, the beauty of a crisp green salad flanking an omelette, embroidered pillowcases that invited one to relax, to rid oneself of tensions, home-tanned sheepskins on shining floors, rows of books each side of a chimney breast, knitting flung down on a leather stool, awaiting fingers to resume their flashing task . . . bottling the bounty of the orchards, ruby-red plums and golden peaches, slivers of pale pears, pickled walnuts, *sauerkraut* and red cabbage. Wasn't it odd . . . some girls married young and chafed against what they thought was dull domesticity. Certainly one ought not to make that the be-all and end-all of life. One needed other interests, to take one's place in community life, keeping one's mind green with news media, reading, most of all reading. . . .

Theresa had a vision of what she'd dreamed of once, what had been within her reach when she had been twenty-three and Murdoch's emerald had been heavy with promise on her finger. Murdoch and herself in their own home, a large house because they planned to have at least four children, and he would need a study. They would have it lined with books, like the study at the Kotare Rectory where Murdoch's father had lived when Theresa was a small girl at primary school. She and Murdoch had had the run of the books in that study because Mr. Gunn had one wall devoted entirely to children's books. Murdoch had been very kind to a small girl who always read books too old for herself, was always running out of reading material, and frequently had nightmares because her reading was too advanced.

She'd always thought that somewhere they'd find a house like the Rectory, even if it wasn't likely they'd ever get one with as fine a view, perched on King-fisher Hill, overlooking Moana Kotare, which meant the Lake of the Kingfisher. Not because so many *kotares* visited it, but because its waters had a peculiar bluish-green tinge, like the feathers of the king-fisher. It had a little path that wound up through the plantation of larches on the hill to skirt the valley and then drop down to the gem of them all, a tiny lake that lay like a dewdrop in the dimples of the hills, and mirrored reflections on a tiny scale that were so perfect they were unbelievable. Lake Iti-whakaata . . . the Lake of the Little Reflections. It was so dear to Theresa. So much of the scenery here was almost too rugged and large for comfort. In this land of tumultuous waters and huge mountains, range upon range, far as the eye could see, it was so endearing to come upon this pocket-size lake, set in miniature hills. It was intimate.

There were no holiday houses at Iti-whakaata, be-cause the land all round belonged to Hamish Macdougall, and while he had an access gate for fishermen, for the excellent brown and rainbow trout in its waters, it was still private. The path from the Rectory was the only other one that led to it and they had never abused that privilege.

Trudi seemed to grow stronger and more like herself every day, but it wasn't till Theresa was assured she had really picked up, that she took her first walk down to the main street of Ludwigtown. She revelled, as always, in the unmistakable goldmining atmosphere, walking under the huge chestnuts and beeches and oaks.

People greeted her gladly as she went her way, her big market basket on her arm. There would be fish in today, brought from the coast in a refrigerated van. Soles from Dunedin, renowned for their flavour and, if she were lucky, some smoked eel for Trudi.

It was in the butcher's shop (where the fish was also sold) that she heard an item of news that puzzled her. Mr. Merriman slipped the sole into a polythene bag, twisted a tie round the top, said, "Are you going back teaching at the High? There's a vacancy, which I suppose you know?"

She nodded. "I may not get it, of course, but I did apply. If not, do you happen to need a cashier?"

He chuckled, "No, but you'd have no trouble getting in at the guesthouses. The tourist season starts earlier every year. And they're never manned fully till Varsity closes and the students come up for jobs. But you'll likely get Miss Rudyard's position. She had to go so suddenly. Her mother was taken ill up in Auckland. Going to be a few changes, what with a new rector and all."

Theresa stared. "New rector? But — but that won't be till next year, will it? Isn't he building next year? He's not very ill, is he?"

"Well, he's being very wise. Far too many men go on too long. Retiring a year early could add a score of years on to his life. That's what I said to him. He did think he'd make it to the end of this year. Only natural he wanted to do that when he made such a good recovery earlier, but the last term's the toughest. So he's wise to down tools. After all, no one's indispensable, and good people are scarce."

Theresa said, with real dismay, "Oh, you mean he's not coming back this term at all? Oh, how horrible! I'd so looked forward to the chance of teaching under him again. That is, if I get the position. Oh dear, this is selfish of me. Of course he ought to retire right away if it's a matter of health. I expect the Deputy Principal will be Acting Head till the end of year, then?"

"Could be, but I've an idea they thought there was a chance of getting someone sooner than that. In fact, someone on the School Board told me, so it seems likely."

Theresa stared again. "You mean the position's already been advertised in the *Gazette?*"

"Aye. Do you want some fish pieces for Ferdinand, Theresa? I've got some quite choice bits here."

Theresa came out feeling all mixed up. If it was common knowledge in the township, how come Dad and Mother had been so indefinite? Or had she misunderstood them? She'd certainly thought they meant the Guthries would be building *next* year on this section they'd bought, and the Rector retiring at the end of it. How odd.

She heard someone say, "Oh, hullo, Tess. I heard you were back and was going to give you a ring." One of the librarians, Maida Shaw. They chatted for a few moments. Maida said, "Any chance you're coming back to the school? My youngster said when she heard you were back that she'd just love to have you for German in the Sixth Form next year. You know what kids are — she took it for granted you'd come back to the High, when she knew that position was going."

"I applied from over there, but it's in the lap of the gods whether or not I get it. If I don't I'll take a job in the township. I feel Trudi needs me."

Maida hesitated, then said, "Look, I heard to-day that the Rector's home. Why don't you call and see him? You must want to know if you've got the job, and he might be free to say who's coming as rector now. Better to come from him than from me."

Fair enough, but she wouldn't ask. If he volunteered the information that would be a different thing. Also, she wouldn't let herself wax sentimental over visiting the Rectory. She'd just better get used to it and not think back nostalgically to the days when Murdoch was the son of the Rector and she came and went as she pleased.

The Rector's wife was delighted to see her. "Robert was wanting to see you as soon as possible. He was going to ring you to ask you to come over. He's much better than before the holidays. Nevertheless, it's a great relief to both of us that he can retire sooner than he hoped, and that things are settled. I was scared he'd insist on staying to the end of the year otherwise. But now someone can actually take over shortly after the commencement of term he's more relaxed."

Just the same Theresa saw a much greater difference in Mr. Guthrie than she had in Trudi. He grinned at her, "Oh, come in. I was going to ring you tonight. I don't mind telling you it's a load off my mind to know you can fill this gap in our staff. Someone I know and trust."

She said, "Oh, I've got it?"

"Yes, your application got here in the nick of time. It couldn't have worked out better. These things do ease one's mind. Bad luck for Miss Rudyard that her mother took ill, but though she's improving, she'll need someone living with her for some months. Come along to the school about three days before start of term and we'll discuss classes, time-tables and so on. I'm going to be very happy to leave a full staff. It's never easy to take on a principalship, and it's the very devil if there are staff shortages. Everyone gets overworked and touchy. Teachers need every one of their free periods — so-called — for preparation for other classes. Otherwise they work round the clock, using all their own time to catch up on things. If a teacher's dedicated, you can't hold him — or her — back, but it can be exhausting. I like to think they can strike a happy balance."

Theresa looked at him indulgently. "Mr. Guthrie, look who's talking! You put so much of your so-called spare time into your job the whole time you've been here, it was positively inspiring. I didn't realise it as a pupil, but the two years I was on the staff I certainly knew it. We won't want any of these way-out types with slack discipline."

The next moment she was aware that Mr. Guthrie was gazing at her in silent astonishment. But why? She began to feel uncomfortable and embarrassed.

He gave a short laugh, said, "But of course it'll go on in the same tradition, with the same discipline. Murdoch's a good chap."

A chill ran over Theresa. No! Oh, no. Please God, no. Then she gave herself a little shake. How stupid could you be? Murdoch was a Scottish surname as well as a given name, and therefore as common in Otago and Southland as most Scottish names were. In fact she knew one rector called that, in Christchurch.

She said, "You — do you mean Hugh Murdoch? From Christchurch?"

The Rector sat bolt upright. "Theresa, you must have known. I mean Murdoch's been in Austria. Your mother told me he was going to see you in Salzburg some time ago. I didn't think it would be easy for you, when I got your application, coming back to a school where the man you used to be engaged to was the new rector, but knowing you'd recently met, and that you're both sensible people, I thought you must have talked it out. Anyway, these days even ex-wives and husbands seem to meet. Why on earth didn't he tell you? Why didn't your people tell you?"

Theresa, had she known it, was white to the lips. She closed her eyes against the impact of it, the increasing awareness that there had been some very dirty work at the crossroads.

She said, through dry lips, "He didn't say a word. I got a letter from Mother saying Grandmamma was talking of going into a Home in Invercargill, that she couldn't live alone any longer and that she was worrying herself sick about Mother having to run two homes. The same day I had a letter from Gwenda Lloyd saying there was a vacancy and enclosing an application form in case I'd had enough of overseas travel now. I told Murdoch that very day, the day of his arrival in Salzburg, and he didn't say a word. Not one!"

He leaned forward and patted her knee. "Child, bring a bit of reason to bear on this. Be fair to Murdoch. He may have been as dismayed as you were. It must have flashed across him that knowing this, you wouldn't have applied for it, and he'd know you had need of this job, and that Trudi had need of you. That would be his reason. I expect he'd been going to tell you immediately. I'm sure that's why he cut short his London stay. He'd always wanted to see Austria, of course, because of the strong Austrian connections we have here in Ludwigtown, and he'd want to see the rest of Europe too, but I'm sure he came to Salzburg especially to tell you."

Theresa choked back all the hot words that were just about spilling out of her; she mustn't. Mr. Guthrie wasn't well. It would upset him. He'd hate to think there might be antagonism flowing between the new Head and one of his staff. How she managed it she didn't know, but she produced a smile, said, "Oh, of course. He wouldn't know how I would have reacted, and would think just that, that I was needing a job here. Sorry about my little outburst. Do forgive me. It won't matter to me a bit, having him as rector, but he wouldn't know that. I won't let it make any difference to my school dealings with him, I promise you."

There was one question she wouldn't ask, but he told her.

"Murdoch will be here in about two or three weeks after term commencement, to take over."

So soon, so soon! About a maximum of twenty-one days. But at least it would give her time to get adjusted to a new job, the timetable, the pupils, to caring for Trudi, for presenting an uncaring front to those who would watch her reactions and Murdoch's with the greatest interest.

She let herself out of the study by the side-door, and looked back, for some reason at the Rector. He was looking after her with a faintly amused and indulgent smile on his face. It made Theresa decidedly uneasy.

It wasn't a case of the grapevine not functioning . . . in a community as small as this, it was as speedy as jet travel. There had been a conspiracy of silence against her? And who . . . *who* had been concerned in it? A good many people!

CHAPTER FIVE

THERESA walked home very slowly, her eyes for once blind to all the beauty of lake and mountain and gardens about her.

She was certain her parents had known about Murdoch. About his appointment. But they hadn't said. Even that last letter they had just mentioned about him being in Canada. When she erupted into the home circle, no doubt they had been instantly dismayed. The poor darlings! They'd been delighted to have her home, but when she'd said she'd applied for the position at the school, they must have thought it a hideous complication. They must have rallied quickly, then by mutual and silent consent amongst them, have said nothing at the time. No doubt later they'd warned the boys to say nothing yet. They might even have hoped, for her own sake, that she didn't get the position.

She couldn't go round telling *everyone* she'd only pretended to be in love with Rudi. She couldn't tell even close friends it had been because she'd fallen out of love with Murdoch — that false excuse! It wouldn't be fair to the new rector. And of course the truth would be more damaging still. There must be no hint, ever, that he'd strayed from the straight and narrow.

She made a wry face. She'd have to stand in the regard of the community always as the girl who'd known a brief and wild infatuation for a glamorous figure from Europe, had chased him across the world, only to be ditched by him. Oh, why, oh, why had she ever embarked on that stupid deception? Theresa actually gnashed her teeth.

She went on her way, fuming. But one thing she was going to do, and right speedily, before Brenda came home. She didn't mind the rest of the family knowing she'd no idea when she returned that Murdoch was to be the new rector. They were old enough to keep their own counsel. But Brenda was a pupil at the school. It was menace enough, that fact alone, without the chance of her discussing the whole thing with relish among her cronies. Brenda was a darling, and Theresa adored her, but had no illusions regarding her scamp of a sister.

Theresa walked slowly, planning it in her mind. She would be sweet with her family, tolerant, would gather them together say she realised how they must have felt when she walked in on them saying she had applied for that position at the school, when they knew Murdoch was to be the new rector. That they'd probably thought she would withdraw her application if she knew in time. As it had happened, it had been decided while she was still airborne.

Theresa knew that if she had been told earlier, she *would* have withdrawn it. It would be ridiculous to do it now. It would prejudice the officials against her for long enough and might affect her future career. Because she was going to be teaching for the rest of her life. Other people suffered broken engagements and finally found happiness with second loves. But no one could take Murdoch's place, even if she didn't trust him enough to marry him. It would be hell, knowing what she knew, especially living here in the same town as Anita.

Stop thinking along those lines, Theresa Keith. Main thing is to get it clear in your mind what you're going to say to the family. She looked at her watch. H'mm. The boys would probably be still lingering over their three o'clock afternoon tea. So she'd skirt the lane to Cloudy Hill and go to the Ridge first.

She had assumed right. Mother was just refilling their cups in the big sunny kitchen. Theresa came in with a slightly jaunty air, grinned at them in the most natural manner possible and as she put her basket down on the dresser said, "Well, the cat's out of the bag, folks. Thanks for not telling me right away. I'd probably have withdrawn my application. I've been to see the Rector. I've got the position and I know Murdoch's the new rector. Don't pretend you didn't know — it's all over town. It doesn't matter two hoots to me. Murdoch and I had quite a pleasant time together in Salzburg, though on purely a friendship basis. We aren't sworn enemies, you know, even if I did ditch him. There's no embarrassment between us and anything we felt for each other long ago is just that — in the past, and dead as a doornail."

"There'll be a lot of conjecture at first, I know, especially among the pupils. And with regard to that, there's something I want to say. I don't want Brenda and her pals sniggering among themselves and saying they'd like to have seen my face when I found out Murdoch was to be the new Principal. As far as she's concerned, I want her to think Murdoch told me in Salzburg, and that I was thinking of coming home anyway, when I knew Trudi wasn't well and thinking of going to Invercargill. I think that's the most sensible idea."

She could have laughed at the look on their faces. Surprise turned to — she was sure — admiration. For her commonsense way of taking it.

Her mother said slowly, "Thank you, Theresa. You're taking it as we hoped you might, but weren't sure. It's a delicate situation, and I hope you think we acted for the best."

"Oh, I do. It was quick thinking on all your parts, when I burst in on you." She turned to her brothers. "Though I did think you two had something up your sleeves. You kept exchanging looks — and I'm glad you preserved silence too. Or am I? Certainly I'd rather teach than anything, but if I'd known Murdoch was to be the new rector, I doubt if I'd have had the courage to apply. However, I don't mind as long as Brenda doesn't know."

She was standing in the corner behind the shut door and at that moment it flew open, completely hiding Theresa, and Brenda, her long dark ponytail flying out behind her, erupted into the room.

"Hullo . . . I got the chance of a ride from Oamaru with the Falkingtons. Saved me the bus fares, so it'll go towards my new saddle. I had an aerogramme from Murdoch. He said Tess was practically on her way, so I thought I'd better be on the scene when she arrives, in case any of you botches the whole affair. And as it was *my* bright idea I daren't risk it!"

Theresa's father made an indescribable sound, but it was drowned out. Brenda rushed on, "I told you it would work! She was bound to fall for it, but I didn't dream she'd act quite so quickly. We'll have to make up a pretty good tale about how surprised we are about Murdoch, though."

As she paused, her sister's voice, cold as ice, said into the petrified silence the other four had preserved out of sheer shock, "Oh, you needn't bother, Brenda. I know it all, and it doesn't matter one iota! I haven't a scrap of feeling left for my former fiancé, and he has none for me!"

Brenda recovered with startling rapidity, though for one astounded moment her face had been a study. "Oh, hasn't he?" she said. "Then why in the world did he enter into a conspiracy with me to get you here?"

Elisabeth's protesting, "No! Stop!" was positively agonised, as if it had been wrung out of her. Roderick moved forward in the most menacing fashion, actually seized his darling younger daughter by the ear and said, "March! You've done enough damage. I never did approve of this mad scheme. I'm going to talk some sense into you if it's the last thing I ever do and ensure that not one word of this is ever squeezed out of you by that mad gang you get round with!"

Theresa took a quick step forward, seized his arm, and her voice was the voice of sheer authority, the kind she used when Sixth Form boys tried to have her on. It had always succeeded and did now. "Leave her be. This is *my* affair."

"All right," said Roderick. "Fair enough, it's your life she's playing round with. But that child dramatises everything. To call it a conspiracy is plain ridiculous. She merely wrote to Murdoch a few weeks ago in Canada and said she was sure you were over Rudi now and that he might catch you on the rebound."

Brenda was recovering. A cork had nothing on that child. She said less dramatically but with horrible conviction, "Then why did he chase you clean across the Atlantic?"

"He didn't by any means chase me right across the Atlantic. He dallied quite a long time in London first. And do you know why? Because he wanted to be in Austria at the same time as a very nice Canadian girl he'd met in Quebec. He was going off on tour with her party when I left. She's got cousins living in Oamaru and is coming out here before too long. Now for heaven's sake don't spread *that* around the school," — that was cunning because it would make Brenda take it seriously — "and one hint from you to any of your irresponsible pals that you engineered things so that I applied for that position not knowing my former fiancé was to be the new rector, and I'll get Murdoch to have you on the mat pronto. No Head would stand for that sort of thing. You've only known him as a friend of the family and a brother-in-law-to-be — believe me, as a teacher, let alone a rector, he's pretty grim! Get me?"

"And," said her father, with real grimness, "if I hear you've breathed as much as one word to anyone, I'll cut your allowance clean in half. And probably your ears off as well!"

Brenda made an airy gesture. "Then I'm likely to be on full pocket-money all year. I wish you'd all realise how mature I am now. It happens with children born to their parents late in life, I believe. They're babied at first by the whole family, especially by brothers," she directed a scornful glance at the boys, who'd not as much as opened their mouths all this time, "and they get a shock when, at an earlier age than most other children, long before puberty, in fact,

86

they suddenly become quite adult. Oh, there's Pegasus in the paddock—" She turned to fly out of the door, hesitated, said in a kindly tone, quite like Trudi's, "And Tess, I wouldn't worry too much about this Canadian girl if I were you!"

It wasn't till the following week, when school had started and the blessed routine of school periods and constant preparation of work, and overfull days and the thought-consuming problems that faced pupils and teachers alike had stopped Theresa brooding, that she became aware that not only Brenda had plotted to bring her home.

She'd been so thrilled the way Trudi had reverted to her old self, and had come to the philosophical conclusion that it had been worth all the damage to her own sensibilities, that it gave her another shock. It was in the staffroom too.

Michael Channing had offered her a cream cake at afternoon tea time when their day was over as far as pupils were concerned.

Theresa waved it away. "No, thanks, Mike. I've put on four pounds since coming home. Trudi is doing all the cooking again now and she's merciless. She loves it so much she reverts to thinking she's cooking for a whole family, and while I'm adamant about not having second helpings, she's far too generous with the firsts."

Mike chuckled. "You girls! As if it need matter to you. It would suit you to put a few pounds on."

Theresa said, "That's not it. The thing is one's clothes won't fit if this goes on, so all I can do is restrain my appetite when I'm away from Trudi."

Frances Toddington chuckled. "It works both ways. When your mother went on that diet so successfully, she had to get a whole new wardrobe. Her things just hung on her. Your father said to me that what they'd saved on the grocery bill she'd spent five-fold on new clothes. But he's a sweetie, isn't he? Said it was all worth while. I adore your parents, Theresa, they make me believe in love."

"You must see more of them," said Mike. "I'd a feeling you wanted to be a career girl, Fran, and that won't suit me at all!"

Theresa saw with delight that Frances had coloured to the roots of her hair.

"Watch it," said Chester Lane, the Deputy Principal, "that's practically a proposal, and the staffroom's no place for these scenes of love and passion!"

"I should say not," said Frances, recovering. "I'm quite sure that Mr. Keith would have picked a really romantic spot, far from the haunts of men, like Kingfisher Hill or the banks of the Awhitu."

Remembrance stabbed at Theresa. She'd had the perfect setting for her own proposal. An autumn day when every poplar and oak on Kingfisher Hill was blazing in gold and russet, when the Lake of the Lilliput Reflections was mirroring sky and clouds and Romney sheep and Hereford cattle so perfectly you couldn't tell which was reflection and which was the right-way-up-world. The asters that the farmer's wife had planted under the willows had starred the grass with purple and rose, bellbirds had been ringing a chorus of notes on the wings of the wind, and a kingfisher had been a streak of turquoise and jade as he dived down. The geese that frequented the lake had set sail from the edge in single formation, and they looked like boats, high-prowed like Egyptian shipping on the Nile, and as if carved from pure alabaster.

She hadn't expected Murdoch Gunn in Ludwigtown till the next day and she'd been wandering by the water's edge in happy anticipation because the last month or so his letters had held a promise of a deepening feeling. The last one at the end had been more explicit. It had said, "When you were ten, Theresa-Tess, and I was twenty, we occupied different worlds. It was a big gap. I've waited and watched it closing. At twenty-two and a bit you could know your own mind. Think on this, will you? — Murdo."

Then that day of the little zephyrs, the little reflections, dreaming of a morrow when Murdo would come and surely declare himself, she had heard him calling her name, and turned to see him coming swiftly, if unevenly because of his lameness, down Kingfisher Hill towards the water's edge . . . and her. "Theresa, here I am, a day early."

She had found her feet wouldn't carry her towards him, yet gladness and surrender were in every line of her, she knew, as she stood at the edge, holding out her hands.

He'd taken one look into her eyes, saw all he needed to know mirrored there from his own, and had taken her to him. He'd put it into words afterwards for the sheer joy of saying them and hearing her echo them back, but it had been completely superfluous. That had been a glad, golden day in April. It had been July when the blow had fallen. She put it out of her mind. She was in the staffroom now, enjoying — or had been — the give and take of quip and jest that went on there.

There was always such a marvellous sense of camaraderie here. Hammering out their problems, laughing their heads off over the howlers in the essays, in the English papers, groaning over misbehaviour, sometimes feeling desperate over some unhappy situation a pupil had become involved in, relaxing otherwise, in a way they couldn't in the form-rooms.

But before she could join in again, the delayed truth hit her. Mother had been *dieting*. She wasn't thin with looking after Trudi! She wasn't thin from worry — she had lost weight purposely.

Everything clicked into place. No wonder Dad had tried to march Brenda off before she could give any more away. They were *all* conspirators. It added up. People being surprised Trudi hadn't been well. Of course she hadn't. She'd pretended too, had written that letter with cunning. Mother, with equal depravity, had added to it. Gwenda Lloyd had been roped in, no doubt, and had gladly sent the application form.

No wonder Grace had been flustered, Maida too, about her not knowing who the new rector was. She was glad Grace had sent her off to the Rectory.

It wasn't till that night, in her room, with old Trudi peacefully sleeping in the room next door, that Theresa relived it.

Shortly after they celebrated their engagement, Murdoch had taken a position at Queenstown High School. After the May holidays. At first it had been heaven. It was a matter of only a dozen miles away, and he took up his quarters in the holiday home his parents had built on the shores of Moana Kotare when they moved. He had spent most of his free time at the Ridge, or at Cloudy Hill. They were planning a January wedding, in the long summer holidays, flying to Austria, where the mountains would be white with snow.

They included Geraldine in many of their outings, naturally, because Theresa didn't want her to feel neglected. They had been a happy threesome, often four, or more, as others joined them. Geraldine was never short of an escort, anyway, though she never seemed to stay serious about anyone for long.

Suddenly Gerry had become a little distant, vaguely preoccupied. Theresa had asked her several times if anything was wrong, but Geraldine always said no.

Naturally there were quite a few evenings when Theresa and Murdoch were apart. Occasionally they studied together, or prepared work, but sometimes they found that too distracting. But it made their free time doubly precious.

Then had come that horrible evening when Geraldine had come over to the Ridge homestead, and they had gone up to Theresa's room to discuss the coming wedding. Theresa had been in Queenstown after school and had brought back samples and patterns for bridesmaids' dresses. She'd sensed that Geraldine's heart wasn't in it.

Suddenly she said, "Gerry, what's wrong? Something's up. You're all nervous, and absentminded."

Then, suddenly, "Oh, Gerry, what is it? Someone you've met? And fallen for? And it's gone wrong — so all this talk of someone else's wedding is upsetting you? Tell me, I'm your best friend, remember?"

Tears had spilled out of Geraldine's eyes. "It's so dreadful when it's your best friend, to have to be the one to tell her. But I must. I mustn't be a coward, whatever difference it makes between you and me. You're so trusting and so happy and I—" She had put her hands over her face.

Cold fear clutched Theresa. She'd said calmly, nevertheless, "Just tell me, Geraldine. Spill it out, get it over. Trusting, you said. Trusting whom? Not — you can't mean — Murdo?"

Geraldine had looked up through her tears and nodded. "I can't stand your not knowing, Tess, because — well, you know what my father was like. How my parents' marriage split up because of it? Mother was warned about him, but she thought he'd reform, after. But he didn't. It never works."

Theresa had gazed at her unbelievingly, almost wanting to laugh. "Your father? But — but that was other women. Not Murdoch. He waited for me all those years — he told me. Waited for me to grow up. He didn't have to."

Gerry had said slowly, "Tess, there were always other women. Not that he wanted to marry any of them. They weren't quite his class. Not his intellectual equal. Not the type for a future rector's wife. That's what he'll have in mind, of course, because he's headmaster material, isn't he? But a complex character. I'd never have told you, if I thought he'd let them all go once he was engaged to you. But to carry on like this, here, under your very nose. I just can't bear it for you."

Theresa uttered that disbelieving laugh again. "Gerry, this is Murdoch you're talking about. You've got to be jo—" But she had stopped under the impact of the pity in Gerry's eyes. She tried again. "But who on earth is he—"

"With Anita Tynedale. Of course she's fascinating. And more Murdoch's age, but how he can—"

"Anita — why, she's married!"

"Well, sort of. It's more than a year since Nort walked out on her. Perhaps there was more excuse for it than we thought. Perhaps there were others before Murdoch. Or perhaps it's been going on for longer than I guessed."

A medley of feelings had assailed Theresa. In face of Gerry's wretchedness, she couldn't feel furious with her, though. "But, Gerry, it doesn't make sense. What possible grounds have you for thinking this about Murdoch?"

Gerry had looked devastated . . . "Oh, I've suspected for long enough, but I didn't want to believe it. But little thing after little thing got forced on my notice. Then lately there've been a lot of incidents. And this week — well, it was too much. He's not been over here much at all this week, has he?"

That struck home. Of course Theresa had been so busy herself. She had also been very understanding about all Murdoch had to do. He'd said whimsically not long before, "If it wasn't that we want that honeymoon in Austria and need the long hols for it, I'd say get married now, when at least we'd be under the same roof doing our prep."

Gerry said, "I couldn't believe it at first either, despite the yarns I heard about him in Oamaru. But this finished me. I saw him *twice* coming away from Anita's very late at night. Once was the night I was here and you said he was at a parent-teacher meeting in Queenstown. Remember how late I stayed? Oh, how glad I was I hadn't allowed you see me part of the way home. He came out of Anita's gate after midnight. She came to the drive entrance with him, they were under the chestnuts a long time. I tried to tell myself there might be some very good reason for it, that perhaps Anita had heard strange noises and sent for him — but I couldn't really come up with anything feasible. The second time, quite frankly, I felt sick. I don't want to tell you every last detail about that. As far as possible since, I've kept tags on him. Remember that night you typed out all those poems for him so he could just run them off on the Banda next morning? He was with her that night — though he'd deny it, of course. And you had more than enough to do that night for your own work!"

Theresa said dully, "I'm afraid I just can't take it in, Gerry. I'll — have to think about it."

Gerry said, "Don't let him think you're a sucker, that you were soft enough to believe in him. It would do Murdoch good to know not all women are easily deceived. It would serve him right if you jilted him without giving any reason except that you don't want to marry him any more. I loathe men like him — putting up a façade of model behaviour and playing the devil behind the scenes. He'll think you'll make him a good wife, but will continue having more erotic experiences on the side."

Nausea had struck at Theresa then. These things only happened to other people, not to her and Murdo. Geraldine had caught at her hands. "Promise me you'll do nothing rash — I mean like confronting him. Oh, I could flay him for treating you like this! I'd like to see him paid back in his own coin. I'd like to see him dumped in favour of someone else. Only that's not possible, really. But perhaps you could pretend you've met someone else."

There'd been a lot more of it with, oddly, Theresa in the role of comforter. No doubt she'd admire Geraldine for it later. It must have been the hardest thing she'd ever done.

Theresa had spent a sleepless night, till at dawn, cold and cheerless at that time of year, she'd got up and gone out for a walk. Anything to clear her head for the day's teaching. As if drawn by a magnet, her feet led her, with horrid fascination, to the hill above the cottage where Anita and her children lived. She just didn't believe it. No. The cold light of day, stark and revealing, had swept away from her brain those

93

fettering cobwebs of doubt and suspicion. It was as simple as that. She'd ask Murdoch about it. She wouldn't say who told her, merely that someone had linked his name with Anita's. Was it true he'd been seen coming out of her house twice, late at night? If so, why?

Theresa stood on the little path among the pines and looked through their dark branches. Then it happened. She thought after it must have been meant to be, to show her a way. The back door of the cottage opened, and someone came out and stood on the step.

No, not *someone* . . . Murdoch!

He turned, called a goodbye, she thought, to someone just inside, called back, "I'll see you tonight, Anita," and hurried along the back path, past a fowl-house and a row of apple-trees, opened a small gate in some cyclone netting and took the right fork of the very path Theresa herself had used, but away from the pines.

It led, in secluded fashion, to the row of holiday homes round this end of Moana Kotare. Where Murdoch's people's holiday home was. The place where he'd been living since he took that position at Queenstown. How very convenient! Two back entrances. If Murdoch hadn't used the front one twice lately, Geraldine wouldn't have seen him and Tess would still have been in foolish, starry-eyed ignorance.

The next day, without saying why, she told Geraldine that she believed her. It was so foolish, subsequently, to feel that stab of disillusionment every time she met her friend. To feel resentment. It wasn't fair to Geraldine. But hadn't someone, somewhere, said the wounds of a friend were hardest of all to bear?

It had been an unworthy relief when Geraldine's mother in Wellington had been taken ill, and she had gone away. She'd spent her time between her parents for years. First a holiday with one, then with the other. Poor Gerry, no wonder she had few illusions left.

Gerry said to Theresa before she left, "When are you telling him you're giving him up?"

Theresa felt as if icy fingers tightened on her throat. "As — as soon as he's got his term exams over."

Gerry had looked astonished and disapproving. "Well, for heaven's sake! How much consideration does he deserve? He's not going to be exactly broken-hearted, you know. Only piqued, stung in his pride. Anita will be able to console him."

Theresa said quietly, "I must do this my own way and in my own time."

Gerry said, "I wish I didn't have to go. I'd like to have stood by you at this time."

"I'll manage on my own, thanks. Don't worry. And thanks for telling me."

Gerry bit her underlip and stifled a sob. "I knew it would make a difference between us. But I felt I must."

Theresa made herself put her arms round Gerry, "Gerry, forgive me. Later it won't matter so much. At the moment I'm not myself. But when it's over and done with I'll thaw out. Give my love to your mother and best wishes for her recovery. Bye-bye, pal, and don't fret."

Theresa had known exactly what she was going to do. Coronet Peak was white and glittering still, for even now, late July, they were still having falls of snow. It was predicted that it would continue much later this year. She would go up in the snow sports bus tomorrow, Saturday, to see Rudi. Rudi who'd made a rueful remark about what he'd like to do to bring his Lisa back to him. "She's always thought I'd be round to fall back on. I'd like to take a New Zealand girl back with me. If only I could find one wanting an Austrian holiday, and being sport enough to pretend!"

Theresa was going to tell him that here was the girl wanting to go to Austria, here was the girl who had enough money saved for her air fare over. She wouldn't need a return. Thank goodness she hadn't got beyond samples for a wedding dress, for Geraldine and Brenda's dresses. And to the devil with all these finer feelings about letting Murdoch get his exams over. What did he care? Rudolf, she was sure, would jump at this. And, of course, he had.

CHAPTER SIX

NOW THE wheel had turned full cycle, she was back in Ludwigtown and — incredibly — Murdoch would be here in four days' time . . . and her boss!

She wasn't going to confront her parents and Trudi and the boys with the fact that she knew they had all conspired. She was suddenly heartachingly sad for them. It must be the very devil to be a parent and see your daughter make a fool of herself. As they'd thought at first, seeing her apparently falling for an Austrian ski instructor, a friend of Tante Evelina's. Then no doubt they had suffered with her and for her again, thinking Rudolf had jilted her, then, with the hopefulness of an older generation, had decided if she and Murdoch were both in Ludwigtown again, the breach might be healed.

They had done it from the best of motives, which was usually a pathetic excuse for something gone hideously wrong. The little jilted one, creeping back home, presumably, as Murdoch had put it, to lick her wounds. Her non-existent wounds! Must have given the family a shock when she told them she'd given Murdoch up simply because she didn't want to marry him. But they would still hope, would trot out that twaddle to each other that she and Murdoch were made for each other all along and that the course of true love never did run smooth. Ah, pah!

And Murdoch himself — what had it been, that offer, that prosaic offer to make it up? She thought it must have been because he wanted to come to Kotare High School as a married man. Oh, it was better for any Principal. Murdoch was thirty-five. Most women of his age, as he'd said, were married by now. There might have been a bit of wounded pride there, being given up for a glamorous Austrian, one who wasn't a lame man. Whatever had been his reason, it wasn't love. Not as she understood it, anyway.

So it was just four days to go. Theresa was as taut as a fiddle-string. She'd be glad to have it over, to plunge into the awkward situation knowing everyone, from the township people to staff members, would be watching their first encounters, discussing them later, telling newcomers the story of how Theresa had fallen for a ski-instructor who had later married someone else. Oh, it made one feel such a fool!

Worst of all would be that gruelling first assembly, with five hundred and sixty-eight pairs of juvenile eyes continually switching from Murdoch to her and her to Murdoch.

This week, thought Theresa as she prepared to leave school, picking up the inevitable heavy satchel of books, is my last without the reality of his constant and irksome presence. Her way took her past the Rectory. She'd not enquired at all about what arrangements were being made for him. If he was going to move in there immediately? How he would manage as a single man? When he would furnish it? She just didn't want to know.

Theresa turned the corner and began to pass the Rectory garden. It was set back into an angle of Kingfisher Hill, built high on the slopes to give the view of Moana Kotare. The lower storey was warm brick, the upper white roughcast, and it was all gables and towers, with an orange tiled roof.

Beautifully designed, it was a family house with small stairways leading to the towers or gable rooms, ideal for hide-and-seek, with odd porches suitable for playrooms or hobbies rooms. Large, yet on the whole quite convenient to run because in such excellent order and had been well designed to save housekeeping footsteps.

The garage was at street level and as Theresa went to pass it, a woman with her arms full of books almost collided with her. A moment for each to step back to avert the collision, then a cry from each of them. "Tess!" and, almost unwillingly, her own greeting, "Mrs. Gunn!" Murdoch's mother.

She was heartachingly like Murdoch. Tall, with an erect carriage and a certain young-hearted eagerness. The same chestnut hair, only with wings of white each side and dark eyes, long and narrow, under brows that in her case were beautifully arched, not beetling over. She had a line of chin that gave charm and character to her face and high cheekbones beneath fanned-out laughter lines at each side of her eyes.

The books slid and tumbled. She said, "There! That was inevitable. James said I was carrying a lazy man's load. Better to take two smaller ones and go more quickly and safely. Aren't men wretchedly logical? How are you, dear?"

She gave Tess a bear-hug, then peered at her. "Much too thin, but like all the girls, dieting I suppose. But how lovely you look in that. We always loved you in green — and your hair is like spun honey. You look good enough to eat. I'll call James." He came out of the garage, a reasonable pile of books in his arms.

There was only the faintest hesitation before he leaned forward and kissed her. Theresa noted it and understood. Hetty Murdoch was so warm-hearted and so able to see everyone's side of any difference, she couldn't alter towards her son's ex-fiancée, but Theresa had heard James had taken it very badly. And she had loved him so dearly. It had been part of the price.

He said the usual things, but his eyes were wary. Theresa was sure he could have throttled his wife when she said, dumping half her load into Theresa's spare arm, "Take these up for me, will you, Tess? That'll save James here growling at me all the way up the path as I drop one book after another."

It would have been churlish to refuse. Theresa pulled a mock-rueful face at Mr. Gunn, hoping he'd understand from it that she would rather be on her way, but was being swept into it. She just prayed no one from the staff saw them. They took the path that meandered through the shrubbery and up some natural stone steps in through a side door in a corner room that was the study.

Theresa stopped still at the sight of the transformation. The Gunns must have been working hard the past two days or so. The walls were lined with Murdoch's books, so many of them dear and familiar to Theresa; his cricket cups were polished and shining on the mantelpiece. The rack for his fishing-rods was fixed to the wall, the old, genuinely antique leather globe Theresa had given him for an engagement present was in a corner, the two winged armchairs from his study at Waianakarua College were in position, a couple of neat steel files were lined up against a wall and his desk and swivel chair occupied a well-lit alcove with a window on the left that gave him an excellent view of anyone making their way up the drive, and a stack of pictures stood against the wall, backs to the room.

Hetty said, "We'll leave him to hang his own pictures. I think it's so irritating if anyone else does it for you. I had to resist a temptation, as it was, to put everything in the places where we had them during all those years in this Rectory. Dump those on that table, will you, Theresa, and come and see the rest of it. And we'll have a cup of tea shortly. Murdoch will have to buy a good deal of furniture, of course, but we got his things from Waianak sent up, and I brought a fair bit of stuff up from the cottage to start him off. He wrote saying he'd prefer to camp in the Rectory. He'd relax more that way, rather than in someone else's house. We're staying in the cottage just now, but we're leaving before he arrives. We've got tenants moving in for a few weeks. Come and have a look."

Willy-nilly, Theresa followed her. Murdoch's mother said, "He'll probably switch things round to suit himself, but it will start him off. I didn't want to put him in his old room — he might feel more like a schoolboy returning than the new rector if I did — and I didn't feel like putting him in the master bedroom — a chap would rattle round in it by himself, it's so huge — 'Theresa flinched inwardly' — so I made it the single spare room — look!" She flung open the door.

Very much a bachelor's bedroom.

Hetty whisked her into the daffodil-yellow kitchen with its grained wood cupboards and stainless steel working surfaces, the efficient-looking electric stove, the big deep-freeze that was permanently installed.

Theresa said rather tonelessly, "Are you going to come up later and housekeep for him, Mrs. Gunn? He'll need someone. His will be such a responsible job. But housekeepers are so hard to get, though I suppose they like the sole charge ones better."

"No, I'm not housekeeping for him, Theresa, even if James and I are free now. It looks as if one is trying to mother a man that way and it's not the right image for a rector — emphasises his lack of a life partner. Besides, James was rector here so long, he might get involved. People drag you in if you want it or not and it would somehow take from Murdoch's stature. I'm not even waiting here to greet him. I've managed to get Martha Hallows to housekeep for him. She's thrilled."

She stopped, said, "I'm prattling. That's because I'm nervous. I've been wanting to see you, darling, because I know this situation is going to be very awkward for you, so I was glad to see you today. I meant what I wrote you, you know, when you broke it off with my son — that it wouldn't alter my feelings for you. I loved you as a child, and what happened between you and Murdoch is your business, not mine, and I couldn't bear there to be any awkwardness between us."

To her horror Theresa felt the tears well up. She dashed at them impatiently with the back of one hand.

Hetty's eyes filled too. "These things happen. I'm not blaming you one iota for falling for Rudi. Life has a way of sweeping us about. I wouldn't be human if I didn't hope that this situation might bring you together again. You've always seemed so right for each other. I find it so hard to believe that you both don't still—"

Theresa put out a hand and stopped her. "Mrs. Gunn, just a moment — you think, naturally, because it's what I wanted everyone to think, that I fell in love with Rudi and he jilted me over there. I was never in love with him. I broke it off with Murdoch for quite different reasons." She flushed deeply. "I'm afraid I don't want to go into those. They were strong reasons, private to me. But I snatched at the chance of going off with Rudi to Austria when the season ended here. It was for Rudi's sake I pretended I was in love with him. He wanted to make Lisa jealous. It — it sort of saved my face."

A voice broke in, "But it didn't save mine, did it, Theresa Keith?" Murdoch's voice. And he sounded as if he hated her.

There was no pity in Murdoch's face for her evident distress. It was as hard as a block of granite. He repeated, when she didn't answer, "It didn't save *my* face, did it, Theresa? I *was* the jilted one, remember?"

How self-righteous he was! It would serve him right if she hurled her real reason at him, in front of his parents, flung it at him that he'd played fast and loose with a married woman while engaged to her, but she couldn't. She couldn't bear to disillusion those two fine people who were his parents. And why rake up the mud now? Let Murdoch Gunn sound justly angry, she couldn't strip him bare. That could be all behind him now; and to the community here must be above reproach.

So she kept silent because she didn't know how to answer.

Murdoch said, "Maybe it's as well I flew in a day early. Didn't expect to find my former fiancée and my mother in cahoots! Sorry, Mother, this isn't much of a greeting after all my time overseas, but I don't want Theresa worming her way into your affections again! The whole thing is wound up, finished. Theresa and I tidied up the ends in Salzburg. We each get a new start, entirely free of each other. Pity it had to be here, in the same place, same school, but we'll make the best of it. Only I don't expect to find you hanging round the Rectory. If you come with a crowd when I'm entertaining the staff, well and good; I mean only because to leave you out would cause talk, because I want no gossip about us. I'm starting a new life and it doesn't include you — understand?"

Theresa unfroze. Bright scarlet, the colour of rage, flowed into her blanched cheeks. "You must be mad! *You actually plotted with Brenda to get me here!* You knew when you came to Salzburg that you'd got the Rectorship. And when I said I was coming home to look after Trudi, you said nothing about it. If you had I'd never have applied for the job, believe me. What possible excuse can you have for that?"

He shrugged. Theresa could have struck him. He said, "Like I told you. Carried away by meeting you again, I thought we might have resolved our differences, returned here together. I was willing to pick up the pieces, put them together again — I even thought I could help you, seeing I knew what it was like to be jilted. Thought I'd patch you up after Rudi dropped you. And," his mouth twisted a little, "I'd have been better pleased to have come back here as a married man. But even then you couldn't be honest. You had to concoct that tale about Rudi asking you to pretend you were in love with him. Really! So I finished up being damned *glad* you didn't take up my offer!"

"Murdoch!" The protest was wrung from his mother. "That's unforgivable! No girl could forgive a statement like that!"

Theresa felt as if her feet were glued to the floor and she was swaying on them. She swallowed, stiffened herself. She was surprised to find her voice sounding so ordinary. "Then just tell me, Murdoch, exactly what you want? How I'm to behave towards you? Because I'll do exactly what you deem right — no more, no less. I'm sorry if my presence on your staff is going to be so embarrassing, but that's your fault, plotting it, before you came to the conclusion that I wasn't worth it. I'd give it up, but there's *my* career to be thought of as well as *yours,* and I don't want to be thought untemperamental and unstable, as I would be, if I suddenly terminated a two-year appointment after three weeks without any valid excuse. So tell me!"

"I want you to behave like any other member of the staff. Some of them already know me, so you can pattern yourself on them, not seeking me out any more than you need, referring to me with the deference due to the position, yet not being subservient, and being natural in the staff room. Mixing — on the surface — because disharmony of any kind can play the devil in a school, and — and this is most important of all — not discussing our former engagement with anyone. Not with staff, friends, relations or by letter with that precious smarmy friend of yours in Canada. Geraldine! She has friends here and she'd report every word you said with embellishments of her own, in letters. And above all, *don't go on discussing me with my mother!"*

Another "Murdoch!" was wrung from Hetty. She said hotly, "My son, you go too far. You're being downright cruel, not to say unjust. *I* dragged Theresa up here. I thrust books at her as I came out of the garage and commanded her to help. I'll see her every time I come up here. You're just my son, not *my* rector, and I'll do what I like. I've always been fond of her and I always will be! She was very ill at ease and I prattled — you know I always do when I'm nervous. And *I* brought up the subject — I've never had a chance to discuss it with her. So it isn't fair to blame her because you overheard us. I can't think what's got into you. You're usually so just, so fair, so tolerant, all the things the Principal of a High School just has to be."

He said sombrely, "I'm not the same man I was before she jilted me."

Theresa couldn't bear the look on Hetty's face. She turned and faced Murdoch, and as she spoke, had

104

she but known, the embarrassment in James's face was replaced by admiration.

"Murdoch, the worst thing that could happen is for any feeling of estrangement to crop up between your mother and yourself. You've always been very close as a family. This was most unfortunate. Your mother, for your sake, I believe, was trying to help. This is the sort of thing you and I have to live down. For some reason everyone — I repeat, *everyone* — seems to think we would make an ideal couple. I'll undertake to disabuse their minds of that idea, if you'll do the same, though not too obviously, on either side. Now I'm going." She put out a hand to Hetty's, touched it briefly, said, "I'm sure once he's got over the shock of hearing us discuss him he'll be sweet to you. I'm sorry it spoiled your reunion. I wish I'd been blunt and said I didn't think it wise to come up to the Rectory with you." She took a step towards the back door, suddenly wanting to cut and run, then said, "Oh, I must get my marking. I put my bag in the study."

She said, irritably, to Murdoch, still standing in the doorway, "Do you mind letting me pass instead of standing there blocking my way, like an avenging angel! You take yourself far too seriously." She went past him, then something bubbled up in her and wouldn't be gainsaid. She turned, took a step back, said, "I don't know that you're as honest and sincere yourself as you were once. You wanted a wife — any wife. I know exactly what changed your mind, after I left. I don't mean *what,* I mean *who!* Catriona Mc-Corkill. And she's far too nice for you!"

He smiled, but there was no amusement in it, only a sneer — and wry malice. "You could be right at that. But I hope you won't tell her so. She's coming to Ludwigtown next year."

Theresa turned slowly about again, walked through the dining-room and the hall, into that study with all his things in it, caught up her satchel and walked out of the door, down the steps and along the little track that wound round the shoulder of Kingfisher Hill towards Ita-whakaata.

And on Monday, she would betray indifference, poise, a sort of splendid unawareness, so her face and her feelings would not betray her in front of that first Assembly.

CHAPTER SEVEN

MONDAY morning came all too soon, yet when she woke Theresa found herself thinking: "Well, at least it's here, and will be soon over."

She knew exactly what she was going to wear. Those Fifth, Sixth, and Seventh Form girls didn't miss a thing. They would expect her to be a little dressed-up. Women usually reacted that way, and they would think she was bound to do so, to meet an ex-fiancé — particularly when someone else had jilted her in the interim. They would think she'd choose something really snazzy in the way of clothes. So she drew out an oatmeal linen pinafore dress that by itself did nothing for her light hair. This morning a dull fawn jersey silk top was going under it and she'd wear putty-coloured shoes.

As she surveyed her colourless reflection in the mirror, she gave a gamin grin. Talk about insipid! She'd simply merge into the background of the others, with her black gown over it, and if she managed the centre of the second row, she wouldn't be half as conscious of those boring, inquisitive eyes.

She heard voices downstairs, cocked her head to listen, grinned again. That would be Mother, here on some flimsy pretext, but in reality to see what her daughter was wearing this important morning and how she was looking.

They heard her coming, she guessed, for her mother slid into saying, as if unaware, "I knew you'd be looking for it, Tru, so thought I'd slip over with it before the work of the day gets under way. Oh, there you are, Tess, I thought you'd be gone by now. Why, Tess, I don't think that's a good choice of blouse, dear. It does nothing for you at all. You need something brighter."

Theresa gave a nonchalant look down at herself. "Oh, do you think so? I thought it was rather elegant myself. You don't want to dress too flamboyantly when you're teaching."

Trudi chuckled, her dark eyes disappearing into slits of mirth. "Well, you've certainly achieved what you are after, *Liebling*. That's protective colouring, like a little fawn bird amongst sand and driftwood."

Theresa managed another grin. "What very bright eyes you've got, Grandmamma! Why, they don't miss a move. I feel exactly like Red Riding Hood, about to be eaten by a wolf. Perhaps if *she* had donned protective colouring instead of scarlet, she wouldn't have run such a risk."

She turned at the doorway, looked saucy, said, "Bye-bye, and don't worry about me, my darlings, I'm getting a certain amount of quite naughty enjoyment out of the situation. Perhaps I'm an exhibitionist at heart!"

It was just as well she did not hear Trudi say to her mother when she was well away, "*Ach,* the poor little one. She whistles in the dark to keep her courage up."

Normally, a new rector would have arrived sooner and had preliminary meetings with his staff, but with coming from overseas, just as the week ended, and not wanting to break into their off-time, he'd only met Chester, the Deputy Principal, so they had been told to be in the staff room half an hour early.

That proved less of an ordeal than expected, because most of the staff were more taken up with appraising the new Rector for themselves, and making an impression on him, than in watching Tess. Four of the staff had known Murdoch before, so it wasn't so noticeable when he greeted Theresa too, by Christian name, and as an old friend. On the surface, anyway, things went off well.

She didn't manage to get the middle seat, she was one in from Michael, the woodwork master, but she was partly screened from view by a huge urn of forsythia Gwenda Lloyd had placed on a palmstand she'd unearthed from the stage props.

In spite of herself she responded to Murdoch's manner, to the meat in his speech. His tone was authoritative, no pandering to popularity here. It rang with confidence, with the knowledge that he was at the helm, that he'd stand no nonsense, yet it was kindly.

"You're not here for fun. You're here to be educated, to be fitted for life, according to your individual talents, to take your place in the community, to earn your living, and I hope each one of you may benefit so much by your schooling here that you'll be able to earn it in the way best suited to your temperament. But I hope we'll have plenty of fun on the side. That makes for a well-balanced life. The core has to be hard work."

"I want you to look on learning as an adventure to be entered upon expectantly every day, not just something to be got over, a dull and irksome duty." He smiled. "There's something I'd like to put over, something one realises later in life, sometimes too late, and that is that the sort of opportunities you have at school don't always occur again in later life. I'd like you to realise here and now that these chances *are* privileges and now is the time to utilise them. Motivation is a great thing. Take languages, for instance. You may detest them, and wonder if they're worth while. It's so easy to drop them and later this is often regretted deeply. We all seem to want to go overseas — New Zealand is a country of potential globe-trotters. Perhaps it's the lure of the faraway, living as we do in the South Pacific and not having the opportunity so many English schoolchildren have, of holidays in Europe, among people who speak different tongues. Most of us return, even if we do have itchy feet, but our travels could have been made much more easy and interesting if we were even a little familiar with languages other than our own."

"To be able to communicate with people is not

only a travel asset, but one in the cause of peace. Here in Ludwigtown we have a head start. Many of our oldest inhabitants may have had sketchy educations due to isolation in the early days, later, to the Depression, but they still have words of other languages woven into their everyday conversation because this was so cosmopolitan an area during the gold-rush days."

"I want your English lessons too, to open up great areas of knowledge before you, through reading, but not only that — I want the school to be the centre of your life, your club, where you play your games, swim, learn to live harmoniously, mainly, but to learn to survive the rough and tumble that is part of it, to become mature enough to cope with the complex pressures of modern life, and though being tolerant of other's problems, to realise that even in a permissive society, true happiness comes from the freedom to choose to obey certain rules. Because there are things this school has always stood for and will continue to stand for, namely . . ."

But Theresa and Michael never heard the end of that. For the last few moments, ever since Mike had called her attention to it by an elbow nudge, they had been keeping an anxious eye on Philip Fordham in the front row, a small First Former. The pallor of his face was dreadful. Was he going to be sick? But usually when Philip's face was ashen, it was because he'd cut himself and was bleeding abnormally.

It was something of a problem. He wasn't a haemophiliac, but some condition of his blood kept it from clotting as quickly as most people's did, and to complicate things he was accident-prone. But he could scarcely have gashed himself during Assembly! Not even Philip! So it must be biliousness. It looked as if Theresa, of all people, seeing she was nearest, with Mike, was going to have to create a disturbance during Murdoch's first Assembly! *Wouldn't* it!

The next moment they realised Philip was clutching his elbow and a second later that blood *was* seeping through his fingers. They acted as one person and very silently. They slid off the corner of the platform, moved to Philip, knowing all eyes would, in any case, be flickering in their direction, and they slid their hands from each side, under Philip's knees and lifted him, gesturing towards the side door with their heads.

Two prefects rose and got it open with a minimum of noise and out they went, followed by the two Sixth Formers who felt this was more exciting than even the Rector's first Assembly.

They got him into the sick-bay, took his coat off. Philip said, "Sorry, I would've seen someone earlier about it, but it happened just as we were going in and I didn't realise I'd got cut. I can't think how, Mr. Channing. One of the boys knocked into me and I fetched up against the bar on the ramp. The bar isn't sharp."

Mike had Philip's coat off and was rolling up his sleeve. "You must have gone with some force. It's burst open, not cut." He grinned at Philip. "Didn't want to miss the new Head, did you?"

Philip grinned back. "No. They said his father was a holy terror, so I wanted to size him up. Gosh, he does look beaky, doesn't he, so I guess he's the same!"

"That will be quite enough from you," said Michael sharply. "We *need* holy terrors here."

There was a step in the corridor and in came the new Rector. There were the usual noises of a tide of youngsters spreading out from the Assembly Hall and going to various rooms, or the sound of their voices as they crossed the quadrangle to modern units.

The Rector nodded to them both, crossed to the boy, lying on the couch, grinned, said, "Won't forget my first Assembly, will you, lad?"

Philip flushed to the roots of his hair. "No, sir. Sorry, sir."

The Rector raised his eyebrows at the coffee. "Not for us, sir," said Theresa meekly, "for Philip. He needs a warm drink with plenty of sweetening. Philip bleeds a little more than most."

He looked down on her, said, "So I see." Her gown had swung open and the front of the pinafore dress was liberally stained. He said, "I'll see if I can get someone to run you home to change."

She shook her head very decidedly. "No, thank you, Mr. Gunn. I've a project I want to get on with during this period without loss of time. They'll be in their classroom as it is. I'll—"

"You can't go into class like that. You might have some squeamish youngster passing out on you."

Theresa said, "I was about to say I'd sponge it off, and pin my gown over the stain. Oh, Mr. Channing, you'll have to do some dabbing too — look, your sleeve!"

Mr. Gunn nodded. He went on asking Philip about his condition, making the boy feel it was more interesting than a handicap. "I'll send my secretary along to sit with you. I noticed on Saturday that she has her work very much up to date."

Work restored Theresa, as she had predicted. It was an absorbing lesson, even when punctuated by the usual disturbances. It was always too much to hope, of course, that every single child would have the right books, the right pencils, pens, rulers. That they had done the amount of preparation they had been told to do, that they would forbear to comment on the incident in the Assembly Hall. They were so cunning; it sounded so solicitous to enquire after Philip. It was an unwritten law that whenever things like this happened, they used it as a diversion as long as possible and had little hope of succeeding because every teacher had also been a pupil once and knew!

Theresa quelled them. They settled down. At lunch-time she heard that Murdoch had visited some class-rooms. Not on a tour of inspection — that would have rattled his staff on the first day — but because certain things had cropped up. She didn't think he'd have any excuse to visit her, but kept even tighter discipline than usual during every period, just in case.

When it came to the last period when she was taking her Fifth Form History class, she began to relax a little. Silly to have been all het up — she wasn't a fledgling teacher, had survived many such ordeals, inspectors and all, and anyway, this particular lesson was interesting because it touched on Germany and Austria, and she'd prepared well for it because she had so much pictorial material to hand as well as first-hand knowledge.

She turned to her blackboards at the side, swinging one forward and scribbling on it. As always when one turned one's back, one was conscious of the class behind. One's ears were strained to catch the slightest relaxing of the work atmosphere. If they were plotting mischief they did it then. So she turned quickly when she heard a noise. She was in time to see George Fielding place his case back on the floor, then became aware that he and two other boys had their cases far too far out in the aisle.

"George! Ramon! Foster! Bring your cases in against your desks this moment! You know they're not to jut out into the aisle. I'm coming down to inspect your work soon. What do you expect me to do? Play leapfrog over them? Or anybody else, pupils included! Why, the new Rector himself might come in. Nice, wouldn't it, if he broke his leg on his first day and History Five were responsible?"

There was an agonised "But watch—" from George, drowned out by the sound of the door opening and of violent contact to the left of and slightly behind Theresa and an involuntary groan.

She whipped round, all too aware that George had been trying to warn her that someone was coming, and that wretched blackboard was sticking out too far, and the next moment she beheld the new Rector positively reeling back, his hands over his eyes.

Theresa herself stood rooted to the spot. Of all the things to happen! As one body the class surged to its collective feet and rushed towards him. Theresa

113

came to life and ordered them back to their seats, "Except for those nearest," she added.

That he had taken a serious crack was obvious. He couldn't speak for the pain. George grabbed a chair and somehow got the Rector into it. Jocelyn said in a tone of sheer authority, "Take your hands away, sir, and let's see the damage!"

The Rector, his cheeks taut and screwed up, did so. Jocelyn said, "No bleeding, no cut, but I'm afraid, sir, you'll have——" She stopped dead.

The Rector managed a grin. "You're afraid I'll have a black eye come morning," he finished for her. He added, "I had the distinct feeling I wasn't expressly welcome in any classroom I've visited so far — but I didn't expect to meet up with such open hostility," and though his hand went up to his face again in pain as the muscles moved, he burst into irresistible laughter. The whole form, vastly relieved, laughed with him. He had them with him from that very moment. He looked at the blackboard, swinging on its hinges, and said, "And that will have its hinges moved to the opposite side before the day is over. It would have been much worse had it laid out, say, an inspector, or the Chairman of the Otago Education Board!"

He sat up a little straighter, took out his handkerchief to hold over his eye, looked across at Miss Keith, who hadn't laughed and who still looked a little sick. "It's all right, Miss Keith. Not to worry. I've had black eyes before — on the rugby field, and twice at cricket, fielding at silly mid-on. You aren't to blame for a poorly designed blackboard unit. I wonder why the builder didn't anticipate just that! One of the newer rooms too. Supposed to be an improvement!"

About three pupils spoke at once. "Sir, it was really our fault." "Yes, she was trying——" and "It was because she was telling us off about leaving our cases out!"

The Rector held up his hand. "I heard, from the

114

corridor. With so much solicitude for my probable progress down the aisle, I certainly wasn't prepared for a booby-trap on entering. However, I'm sure my housekeeper is the sort to believe in the old-fashioned application of a beefsteak to the eye. I can but hope I have no visitors tonight."

The class roared its appreciation again. From now on they'd regard the Rector as no end of a good sport, and he'd hold them in the hollow of his hand. But it wasn't going to be easy to get them settled again. And what a story it would make round every tea-table tonight! History Five would feel they had a head start on every other form in establishing good relations with the new Rector. And she, Theresa Keith, would be known all round the area as the teacher who'd blacked the Rector's eye on his first day! She could just imagine the comments of the fathers! "Oh, well, perhaps she was getting something out of her system. Used to be engaged to him, you know," would be the mildest!

It wasn't long till the end of the lesson. The Rector stayed with them till the last horrible moment. Theresa felt like a wrung-out dishcloth. Then it was over and they were dismissed and filed out in the most orderly fashion imaginable.

Murdoch and Theresa were left looking at each other. Murdoch smiled, though obviously the movement of his face muscles made him wince. He said crisply, "Better rustle up your sense of humour, Theresa, don't take it so seriously." -

She said, "I shall be the laughing-stock of the whole school."

"Rubbish! *You* won't be wearing a purple eye. *I* will be. I don't know why it is, but it's an injury that seems more comical than any other. Come on to the staffroom for some afternoon tea."

Unwillingly she said, "All right," looked up into his face and caught sight of the eye rapidly beginning to swell, locked glances with him and, to her own dismay, laughter bubbled up in her and welled over.

"Much, much better," approved the Rector, when they had both stopped. "I thought if you were going to dramatise every situation that crops up, because of our previous more personal relationship, it would be the very devil."

They were last into the staffroom. There was a buzz of conversation from it as they neared. It died a sudden death as they entered. Their eyes fastened on their Rector's face, then tried to look elsewhere.

Murdoch spoke very naturally. "It's really a good one, isn't it? All done in the manner of the best comedies. She was ordering the boys to remove their cases from the aisle in case I tripped, and I copped the blackboard she left swinging."

But she felt very rueful as she walked home. She'd have given a lot for it not to have happened. She had wanted to impress Murdoch with her air of detachment, her dignity, her efficiency. All that had happened was that she'd given him a black eye and he'd taken her to task for making too much of it. Had told her in effect, not to be so childish, told her to have more poise. Inwardly Theresa writhed over it still, even if she'd laughed with the others. It had all been so undignified. Where was it she had read, long ago, that the things that keep us awake most at night are our humiliations, not our sins. She had an idea it was very true.

She took the long way home, round the shoulder of the hill that overlooked Moana Kotare. From the leafy shade of the English beeches she looked down on the waters of the lake, wind-ruffled and cornflower blue, not a large lake as compared to Wakatipu, but infinitely dearer to her heart, because it belonged to her. Because she could never remember a time when she couldn't see it from the windows of home. Across it rose the triangular peak of Puke-ataahua, which meant, simply, the Hill of Beauty, though in height it was a mountain. A homestead nestled there, served only by launches. To the right swelled the symmetrical double feature of Mahanga-Puke, Twin Hills,

116

and on the left, the slanting levels of the river terraces above Waimangaroa, which meant the long branch of a river. This was the waterway that brought the rain down from the watershed of the ranges deep back in towards the west, to fill Kotare. At the other end the Awakeri drained the lake, joining miles away the tumultuous waters of the Kawarau that functioned similarly for Wakatipu.

Murdo would think she was still the adventurous, impulsive child who had involved him in so many adventures. He'd been very patient with her and Geraldine in their madcap days, rescuing them from the consequences of their escapades many a time and oft. Worst of all had been the time they had been lost on the Macetown Track. Certainly in that case it had been Geraldine to blame, but Gerry had begged her not to say she'd been the one who'd insisted on going further and further despite Theresa pointing out storm-clouds, in a region where the Arrow River could rise to frightening proportions in so short a time.

Even now Theresa could shudder at the remembrance of that terrifying night, spent among hills that flashed and reverberated with a spectacular thunderstorm. It had been Murdoch who had found them the next day, late in the afternoon, still trying to find some place fordable, some smaller gully, where they might avoid the big river and find their way back to Arrowtown. Murdoch had come in the long way round — an incredibly long way — but safer, through Red Spur Gully, up Breakneck Crag and over, negotiating places like Irish Man's Hazard and Ryan's Slip, places that had been fearsome in goldmining days, when they had been constantly used, but now were even more treacherous because of landslips after rain, and the bush that crept back and concealed crumbling cliffs.

It had happened on Pluto's Staircase. Murdo had got them both over a part that was so broken away no natural step remained. He had hurtled over, clutching at everything, into the stream-bed, fortunately where the water did not reach. By the time she and

Geraldine had got to him, he'd been picking himself up and they hadn't known how badly he had injured the leg till he'd got them to the safety of the Drumlogie Homestead and had passed out on them. He'd spent three months in the Dunedin Hospital and it had been thought then his limp would have been permanent.

But now he walked as well as he had ever walked. He was even skiing again. That was something to be thankful for.

This was a lonely part. Solitude was so healing. The blue of the lake, the green of the trees, the sounds of birds calling, all spoke a peace and serenity to Theresa, soothed the nerves the day had set jangling.

By the time she reached home, she was able to tell her mother and grandmamma what a day it had been and to chuckle over it. They were properly horrified to know Murdoch had sustained so painful and prominent an injury, though.

Trudi said, "I want you to find out right now if Martha happens to have any beefsteak in her fridge. His mother was stocking up the deep freeze, but if all the beef was in there, it would be of no use at all. You can't put solid blocks on. And in my own cupboard, right this moment, I have a piece of cornercut of topside I was going to marinate tonight for some *sauerbraten.* I could take a slice off."

Theresa said hastily, "Count me out. *I'm* not ringing. You can, Mother, or Trudi. *And* I'm not taking it over if he does want it. I'm not giving anyone the chance to say I'm hanging round the Rectory."

She interpreted the look on their faces correctly and said, "I'm not being petty. Murdoch warned me against doing just that — told me not to, on Friday. He said he would have me there only when there was a crowd — even said he didn't want me worming my way into his mother's affections again."

She had the satisfaction of seeing them struck dumb. Trudi rallied first. "Well, he'd never be as

118

rude as that to me. That's one of the few privileges of being old. *I'll* ring — and take it over too if he wants it."

He didn't. Oh, no. He didn't need her ministrations either. They heard Trudi say, "Is that you, Martha? No, I thought it was not her voice. How are you, Anita? We have not seen you this long time since."

Anita. Across at the Rectory on Murdoch's first day! They must be mad!

Trudi continued, "Yes, of course, you would hear it from Murray. And you would hasten across with the beefsteak in case they did not have any." She chuckled. "Tell him old Trudi says he is not to behave like a small spoilt boy. That of course it feels horrible, but it will benefit him. Theresa tells us you have a very bright boy in Murray. And how is the wee one, is she quite well? *Ach,* yes, a little darling. And now goodbye to let you get on with the good work."

She replaced the receiver. "Anita is there, with a slice of beefsteak. She gives lectures in First Aid, so he will be well looked after. She is a good girl, that. Takes her place in the community very well. She and Murdoch were inseparable when they were at primary. It is nice to see friendship lasting. She will be most happy to have him Principal of the school her children attend, the son of her own old Rector."

Well, Anita hadn't lost much time. Murdoch wouldn't tell *her* not to hang round the Rectory. They were both very foolish. Not for the first time Theresa wondered how many people had known or suspected. Not many, probably, or Murdoch wouldn't have been offered the Rectorship. She wondered how Geraldine had been alerted in the first place. It would have taken more, surely, than two sightings late at night, outside Anita's cottage. Though Geraldine's reporting of those two had triggered off Theresa's own discovery, which was much more damning. A wave of desolation swept over Theresa. What if Geraldine had never told her? What if she had married Murdoch in ignorance? If it had been a passing infatuation, soon spent? Was ignorance really bliss? She didn't know. Meanwhile, there was work.

This was a busy term, with everything hotting up towards the exams, and pupils really getting down to it. There were fewer social affairs till, of course, the welter of them when exams were all over and the end-of-year functions would be upon them. But the Parent-Teacher Ball was to be a really big function this year, because it would be the first effort towards funds for the new gymnasium, so they could get a Government subsidy.

Theresa found that with the pace of the work and the vast amount of preparation involved, some of the tenseness went out of the situation for her. True, she was conscious many a time of a sudden pang catching up with her, a sense of unreality sweeping her in the banter of the staffroom to think that this was actually happening; she was a member of Murdoch's staff and no more to him than anyone else.

Occasionally he said a word or two that singled them out, but never in front of the others. One day, when he came in just as Frances Toddington went out, he said to Theresa, "You and Fran are very good friends?"

"Yes, Fran's a lovely girl — such fun, and a splendid teacher. She looks so daintily feminine — like the fairy on top of the Christmas tree — but every one of those great Sixth and Seventh Form boys hold her in the liveliest respect."

"That's so. She's an excellent disciplinarian. She'd never let them get away with anything. But they like her tremendously." His face creased into a reminiscent grin. "They call her the Juggernaut."

"Yes, but how did you know? It's usually a case of the Rector being the last to know."

"I overheard it."

Theresa laughed. "They're so careless. The things

one hears in the playground! They must think we're so old we're deaf!"

The Rector nodded. "Though this wasn't at school. I was at Anita Tynedale's. And Murray burst in, not seeing me, saying, "Mum, guess what old Juggernaut said today? The most ridiculous spoonerism—" Then he caught sight of me. I was positively amazed when I heard it was Fran. But it's in the nature of a compliment to her personality."

Theresa turned away a little so he could not see her face. There was one thing — he must never have suspected it was because of his association with Anita that she had given him up.

Murdoch found what he'd left in the staffroom, picked it up, and said over his shoulder as he left the room, "A much more healthy friendship than your one with Geraldine, I'd say."

It was a good job he hadn't stayed. She might have lashed out with something she would have regretted later.

It was a Saturday and Theresa was coming back from the Public Library with a basket of books for Trudi when she came upon Anita, gardening outside her front fence.

She rose when she saw Theresa, a swift smile lighting her face. She was tall and slim and incredibly young-looking to be the mother of a sixteen-year-old boy. But of course she *was* young. Barely thirty-five, Murdoch's age. She was pleasantly mature now with a beauty that was ageless, Theresa was sure. Dark hair that was smooth and almost blue-black, legacy from a Spanish great-grandfather of the mining days, someone who had deserted his ship in Dunedin, to try his luck. A creamy olive skin with a faint carnation pink staining the high cheekbones. She had a bone structure that would have delighted a sculptor, brows and nose curved with symmetry, slightly concave cheeks, a hint of shadowing beneath the eyes that owed nothing to artifice, and a jawline of chiselled perfection. Her eye-

121

brows were winged, never needing plucking, and the eyes themselves were, surprisingly, the sapphire blue of Lake Wakatipu on an autumn day. Exactly as Geraldine had said, too tiresomely lovely!

"Theresa, could you spare a moment? I'm just going in to make myself a cup of tea. Didn't have a chance to see you when you first came back. I was away a fortnight in Dunedin, staying with Murdoch's mother. The girls and Nort and Murray managed fine. I had Inez with me, of course."

Inez, the little one Trudi had spoken of. Anita must have had her after Nort had come·back to her. She'd been' staying with Mrs. Gunn! Odd that Murdoch had never warned *her* off. Much more likely to be gossip there!

Anita continued, "I knew you'd be frightfully busy, anyway, though I've been thinking of ringing to ask if you'd like to come over for a meal. Murray sings your praises. He asked the other day couldn't we have you over. I think it's marvellous when children like a teacher, yet respect her. It makes all the difference to their progress."

Theresa followed her up the path. Anita and Nort kept their large property beautifully. Match-heads formed a solid blue edge to the borders, pink primroses fringed a weeping rose, yellow ones a circular plot where forsythia showered gold, inky-blue ones set pink peach blossom off. A long rectangular bed had wallflowers and forget-me-nots opening and by the look of the buds, tulips would open chalices of scarlet and gold amongst them soon.

It was all, somehow, surprising. Not the garden of a wanton, Theresa thought, and was immediately ashamed of the spiteful thought. An old-fashioned, narrow term at that. Anita had been married so young and Norton was so — what was the word? Not exactly insipid, but rather lackadaisical, savourless. No one could have applied those adjectives to Anita. What adjectives *would* apply? Sultry? Yes, sultry. As if the life-forces, now carefully tamped down and disciplined to everyday family life, just smouldered beneath the surface. Always she had seemed tireless, as if stores of energy — emotional as well as physical, perhaps — were banked up within her. She never seemed to hurry, never flapped.

Had Nort been unable to satisfy her? Had Murdoch's quick wit, his essential maleness, appealed to her? Theresa had a moment of insight. When you were single, looking forward in due time to marriage, but with other things on your mind, your career, your dreams of travel, all sorts of things, what did you know of other people's longings, longings that might have gone unsatisfied, even in marriage? The girls who married young and felt something was lacking. Oh, not all girls. Some were richly satisfied, but what if Anita had felt . . . what? Unfulfilled? Marriage might have awakened in her desires not known before, and still not have reached the heights. There might have been dark moods, tides of emotion hard to resist and, as far as Murdoch was concerned, Murdoch who'd waited a long time for a little girl to grow up, Anita might have suddenly satisfied something in him. She had a poised charm a man could find heady, with the contrast and promise of a full, passionate, sweetly curved mouth.

These thoughts chased through Theresa's mind, and left her feeling spent. She hadn't expected them to come to her. She'd thought she would have been more conscious of something approaching hate and censure.

It seemed so strange to find the conversation so ordinary.

"I'm on my own," Anita was saying. "Nort's got the children over at Queenstown today. He'd promised them a ride up to the Chalet on the Gondolas, and a visit to the Motor Museum. It was such a lovely day."

"What a pity you couldn't have gone, too," said Theresa, her mind instantly wondering why Anita had chosen to stay home. She thought of the million-dollar view from the Chalet, of the lake that was called The-Trough-of-the-Goblin, and thought Anita might have hoped Murdoch would stroll over. She took a grip on herself.

"Oh, the plumber was coming — we had a flood in the cylinder cupboard last night. The children were so disappointed, but I said I'd rather stay and get my plants in, and they know I love gardening, so they went off quite happily. The weather's been so capricious, as always in spring, and the other Saturdays are going to be very busy, so I thought the children might miss out."

Theresa mocked herself inwardly. Not an assignment with Murdoch but with the plumber!

Anita poured the tea. What beautiful hands she had. She could have graced any salon in Europe last century as a hostess, but here she was, in an old cottage, beautifully modernised, in a remote corner of the Southern Hemisphere, and she looked — Theresa was almost sure — immeasurably content and glowing with vitality and . . . happiness?

Theresa suddenly wished she had visited her before Murdoch came home. Was this look Anita had now because of him? Anita had always been exquisite, but now there was that glow, a sort of incandescence. Theresa knew she had possessed it herself during the short months of her engagement.

Anita said suddenly, not bothering with a skilful leading up, "I wanted to tell you, Theresa, that I'm not the same person I was when you left Ludwigtown two years and more ago. I was very bitter and hard, and a few more things then. Because Nort had left me. I came a real cropper over that. I saw myself in an entirely different light. I was — very self-sufficient till then. I even thought I could make a reasonable job of being a solo parent, and I couldn't. I had to sink my pride. I'd not realised I had so much pride. I had to really humble myself before Nort would come back.

"I hadn't known how much harm I'd done his

personality, or how fine he was, how patient and forgiving. I'd made a real mess of things. We made a completely new start, and now — oddly enough — I wouldn't have had our lives any different. When Nort left me and I came to my senses, I used to long to be able to undo the past. But now, even while I am ashamed of some of it, I wouldn't forgo any of it, because it's shaped and moulded me. Isn't it odd, how we learn by our mistakes and even come to the conclusion that wouldn't want it any different, anyway?"

Theresa had an idea this could be the moment of truth. She said, putting down her cup, "Why are you telling me all this, Anita?"

Anita refilled Theresa's cup, and didn't look up. "Because all sorts of things have happened to you too, Theresa — misunderstandings, a ruptured relationship. I'd like to think that you and Murdoch, though you probably won't believe it right now, could easily find yourselves back in square one. Don't be afraid of gossip. Naturally, people are wondering if you and Murdoch may yet marry. I'd love to think you did."

"People do talk. It's a pity, but one can't stop it. Nort and I have had our fair share of it. A broken marriage — or at least a separation — is a target for it. So I expect a broken engagement — and a resumption — is too, to a lesser degree, but don't let it get under your skin. I've been amazed at the things people can bring themselves to say. What hurt me was that Nort was criticised more than I was, and it was my fault. Because he was the one who cleared out and left me with the family, people blamed him. If they only knew! I felt it so badly I wanted to confess my faults to them all, but in a way, that would have belittled Nort more — they would have despised him. As it is now, he's head of our family, his rightful place. It's been the taming of the shrew all over again. One woman even said, 'Fancy taking him back! I'd never trust a man again when he'd been

125

footloose so long.' I almost told her the truth out of sheer indignation, but wiser thoughts prevailed."

Theresa was astonished to find she was feeling admiration, not distress. But she found it hard to swallow her bite of scone. When she had she said gently, "That was wise of you. Thank you for telling me this, Anita. I know how hard it must have been for you. It's taken real courage and I do appreciate it. I take it that you want me to understand that—"

She had been going to say: "That it's all over between you," but Anita interrupted her.

"I want you to understand that pride can ruin your life. I feel you might be too proud to admit to Murdoch that you still — still care. I feel that with everyone conjecturing about the two of you, you could be very prickly with him, not give him a chance."

It sidetracked Theresa. She said hotly, "He doesn't *want* a chance. He told me to stay away from the Rectory, not to worm my way into his mother's affections again."

Anita looked aghast. *"Murdoch* said that?"

"Murdoch did."

There were actually tears in the vivid blue eyes. Anita said slowly, "Then it's *his* pride getting in the way. Don't you see, Theresa, that he still thinks you jilted him for Rudi? I think he doesn't want to be second-best. But you and I both know that that was not your reason for jilting him."

Theresa stared. "What do you mean?"

"Lisa told me. I — I'm so fond of Murdoch, of all the Gunns. I worried about your broken engagement. But there was nothing I could do about it at such a distance. You were in Austria and probably would become engaged to Rudolf. Then suddenly he appeared here, with a different bride. I had to try to find out what was wrong. Murdoch wasn't here, of course — he was at Waianakarua. He only came here very briefly to say goodbye to your people before he left for Canada."

"I liked Lisa. She came here often when Rudi was up the mountain. She was lonely. I let my concern for you and Murdoch show and she came out with it one day."

Theresa swallowed. "Came out with what?"

Anita looked a little surprised. "That the affair — the seeming attraction for Rudi — was a put-up job. That it was solely for Rudi's sake. At least that you used his need to get away from Murdoch. I'm sorry it backfired on you, though, Theresa, so that people murmur things like "Serve her right," because you first gave Murdoch up."

Theresa said, "Did Lisa tell you why? My real reason?"

Anita shook her head. "Oh, no. She just said you'd taken that way of breaking an engagement you wanted to terminate. But I—"

"But you—?"

Anita said, "I happened to be at the Dunedin Airport when you left for Austria with Rudi. I was waiting, with Nort, for the Mount Cook Airline. He'd been in Dunedin. I'd gone to him, asked him to come back to us, to make a fresh start. I was so happy. I felt I hadn't any right to that happiness when I saw your face. I tried to tell myself it was only because you had just left your family back in Queenstown. But it haunted me. I felt you ought not to look — quite like that — if you were going away with the man you loved, to meet his people."

Bitter regret washed over Theresa. It had been as close as that. As she had left Central Otago, Nort and Anita had been reunited and the affair with Murdoch was over.

"When Lisa told me you'd never been in love with Rudi, I made up my mind someone had made mischief." Anita had been playing with the crumbs on her plate, squeezing them into balls and then crumbling them again. Now she looked up directly at Theresa. "Was it Geraldine?"

Theresa caught in her breath. Anita must have

suspected that Geraldine knew. Suddenly she couldn't bear it. But she mustn't let Anita know how badly she felt. She was sorry for Anita, she was so obviously trying to make amends. It must be terrible to have such a thing on one's conscience. The breaking up of two people's lives, especially when one had found new happiness oneself. Suddenly all Theresa wanted to do was to get away from here, from this cottage where Murdoch had loved Anita. So she lied.

"Geraldine . . . make mischief? Oh, heavens, no. Anita, I helped Rudi, yes, but I used him too. I don't want to go into my reasons. It's all dead mutton now. No doubt in time Murdoch and I will marry other people, and none of this will matter. I think, Anita, when I marry, it should be someone nearer my own age. Ten years didn't seem to matter once. I sort of hero-worshipped him. I grew out of it, but—" She reached out a hand and patted Anita's. "I do appreciate this. I rather think everyone thinks we still carry a torch for each other, but that's not so. Oh, is that your family coming?"

Anita pulled a face. "It is. They don't so much come, as erupt in. Here we go!"

Stephanie got to her mother first. "Look what Dad bought you in Queenstown!" She had the paper off and had snapped open the small jeweller's box in an instant. Here lay a *paua* shell pendant, shaped like a star, rimmed with silver, and reflecting all the lights of a kingfisher's wing, delicate and iridescent.

Anita sparkled, "Oh, Nort, how lovely! It matches my earrings and bracelet perfectly. I shall wear them to the Parent-Teacher Ball. Stephanie, look who's here."

The children all greeted her. Rosalie said, "We weren't sorry after all you couldn't come, Mum. It made it more of a surprise."

Murray was grinning. "Mum, what do you think? The girls actually made some intelligent remarks about the vintage cars. Even Rosalie!"

"That'll be enough," said Nort. "You can all go

over to your grandma's now and take her those eggs. They're in that box on the dresser. And bring her wood and coal in. Better get away before Inez comes in or she'll want to go too, and she's dead beat now but doesn't know it. She got delayed with the cat on the way up the path."

The children picked up the box and disappeared, presumably to dodge out of another door. Inez appeared, her small arms full of a very large pussy. Nort bent down, laughing, and picked her up. What an enchanting child! She was laughing too, and looked over the striped head to her mother. "Mummy, we saw some funny ducks. They walked on the bottom of the water."

"Black teal," said Nort. "She doesn't miss a thing. All the other ducks went bottoms up in the shallows, you see. You know how the teal stay down a bit, scuttling round."

Theresa blinked. "Good gracious, what a perfect talker! I've never heard a child so young talk like that." She added, "How old is she?"

"Not quite a year and eight months. None of the rest put sentences together till they were almost two. Her birthday isn't till February. Odd, we thought she'd be quite a lot more backward than the others — she was premature. But once she got to five months she caught up and passed them in almost everything."

Anita added, "Perhaps it's because of the older ones. I believe the youngest often surpass them. They talk to her all the time, and she seemed to be trying to catch up with them from the moment she said Dad-dad."

The cat wriggled and escaped. Nort put Inez on the floor. She toddled across to Theresa, put a fat, starfish hand on her knee, looked up at her trustingly. This child was quite different from the others. She had chestnut hair crisping into tendrils, whereas Murray had Anita's smooth black locks, and the girls had long straight hair like Nort's, almost flaxen. And all three of the older ones had startlingly blue eyes like both parents. This one had dark eyes with tawny glints in them, almost reddish. Theresa lifted her on to her knee, babbled what she felt were inanities and said she must get away.

Anita walked to the gate with her. Theresa was proud of herself, because she felt as if her whole world was falling round her. She managed to thank her, say very naturally that she'd come again, then she walked the long way home to get control of herself. That had never been a premature child! How disconcerting for them when she proved so advanced for her age. It had been August when Theresa had left Central Otago two years ago, when Nort and Anita had mended their marriage. Anita had given birth to Inez in the February. No wonder Anita had wanted her husband back with her! Who did she think she was kidding?

By the time she got home Theresa had pulled herself together. She wouldn't doubt Anita's sincerity, her desire to make amends. She was — quite evidently — a different person now. Norton had forgiven her. They seemed ideally happy and Norton was somehow more lively. He'd been too quiet before.

As Theresa put her hand on the gate to lift the latch, she stopped and pondered. If Murdoch had confessed it to her, how *would* she have taken it? She didn't know. If — supposing he still wanted to marry her — he confessed *now*, how would she take it? She didn't know that either.

She walked briskly up the path, pushed open the kitchen door off the verandah and walked in. Trudi was sitting knitting at the table, Murdoch was sitting there too, eating apfelstrudel, hot and spicy, straight from the oven, smothered in cream!

He couldn't speak because his mouth was full. But Theresa did. "Good heavens! Just look what's surfaced! Not at all calorie-conscious, I see. And did no one ever warn you about cholesterol and hardening of the arteries?"

Murdoch swallowed, grinned, said, "As an example of hospitality that remark is about perfect!"

Theresa put her basket of books down on the table. Not gently.

"What did you expect? The fatted calf? The olive branch? And as far as hospitality goes, might I remind you of your remark . . . warning me not to hang round the Rectory too much? Or worm my way into your mother's affections again! So you can't hope to have red carpet treatment here. It seems to me that telling Trudi that Martha's apfelstrudel isn't a patch on hers could come under the worming-into-affections category."

He was quite unperturbed. "I was never out of her affections."

"Meaning your mother stopped being fond of *me?*"

"Well, *you* ditched *me.* Not the reverse. Mothers often take it badly when their only son gets jilted. You could scarcely expect her to regard you the same."

"Jilted! If I'm not tired of hearing that word!"

"Why, who's been using it lately?"

Trudi went on knitting, her shrewd eyes going from one to the other. Let them have it out. Better than all this indifference.

Theresa thought, well, he asked! and said, "Anita, for instance, just this afternoon."

If he hadn't been scooping up more strudel he'd have seen how intent on him her eyes were.

He didn't react as she thought. It was quite mild. "Anita? What did she have to say about it?"

Theresa's eyes narrowed. She said deliberately, "She thinks she can somehow make amends for her own foolishness by trying to patch up other people's quarrels. Like my little sister, the manipulator of people's lives."

He grew very still. "Patch up our quarrel? *Did* we quarrel? I thought not. A quarrel is face to face. You didn't even have the guts for that. Just left me a note, after giving me an anxious week or two, when

131

I was wondering what had come over you with Rudi."

"There was a very good reason for that. I wanted finality about it."

"You certainly achieved that. But I didn't admire you for it. I thought that something I'd waited for so long, something we ourselves had planned for the rest of our lives, deserved some time, at least, for discussion."

"All right. If it's only the way I did things that irked you, Murdoch, I admit that was wrong of me. I ought to have come out in the open, face to face. But don't be so odiously self-righteous. That's your trouble — you're so much the master of your fate. Which is only another way of saying you trample on other people's feelings. I loathe arrogance and smug self-satisfaction. Perhaps that was a contributing cause. It can appeal to a young girl, makes her feel safe, secure, at first, but it's not to say she wants all that dominance and my-way-right-or-wrong to be what she bestows on her children in the shape of a father. And I realised that."

He'd finished the strudel. He pushed the plate away from him and swung round to gaze at her. He said, "Sit down!"

She sat, automatically, then said furiously, "See what I mean! You say sit and I sit. We aren't on a Principal - teacher relationship now. We're in my granny's house, just two people."

"Of course we aren't on that basis this afternoon. But we weren't then. You were engaged to me. And when was I ever dictatorial, dominant? When did I ever impose my will upon you?"

He had her there. She said hastily, "Well, I could see how it was going to be."

He looked at her witheringly. "You could have talked that out. Made me conscious of my faults. Heavens, girl, married couples have to talk out much bigger issues than that. They admit their faults and start again. Forgive each other — and forget — I've never thought forgiving without forgetting was worth a tin of fish. Look at Anita and Nort!"

Her lips parted, but no sound came out. She couldn't speak. Not in front of Trudi, at the moment, while he was no more to Trudi than the High School boy who'd always been fond of her apfelstrudel, he was still the Rector of that High School. And in any case, Trudi must not be disillusioned.

For the first time Trudi intervened. "Yes, Anita. She was proud, that one, proud of her efficiency, her way of life. She overshadowed Nort completely, till he left her and she realised her own inadequacy. Nort came back to his rightful place in the family. Anita has more friends now. She was so perfection-mad before that that she hadn't many. It's not endearing, too much perfection. Sometimes our very faults endear us to our families. She didn't find true happiness till she admitted hers. I think I should leave you now to talk things over. You need to be without me, an old, done woman, making a third."

Murdoch put out a hand to her across the table. "No, Trudi, stay. This isn't a discussion with a view to reconciliation. It's just that we still strike sparks off each other and we're so damned polite to each other during school hours, it's a relief to slang each other once in a while."

His glance across the table was the sort that scorched evasive pupils when they dredged up ridiculous excuses for poor behaviour. "Theresa, I've known you too long not to know when you're lying, and I knew you were, that day up the Kapuzinerburg."

"I wonder if Rudi and Lisa could convince you."

He banged his fist on the table. "I don't mean that. I know you did it for Rudi."

"Then what do you mean? That was what we talked about under the chestnuts that day."

"I mean when you said you used Rudi as an excuse to give me up."

"Well, I did, didn't I? Give you up, I mean."

"I meant your reason. Not loving me."

Theresa managed a scornful laugh. "How vain can a man get? I don't know how you can sit there in front of my granny and say such things. Have you no idea how that sounds? It's unbelievable!"

He didn't reply. His silence goaded Theresa. "And what do you want to know for now, anyway?"

"Oh, not because I want to rake over old ashes. I may have thought, in Salzburg, that it might serve, thought we might make a go of things after all, that fundamentally we were the same people we were once. No, Trudi, don't go. This isn't a quarrel ready to be made up. It's just a discussion. Too much water has flowed under the bridge by now. We're both changed. But when a chap has offered the rest of his life to a girl and she's accepted him, I think he ought to know the true reason why she changed her mind. In fact, if he met another girl and wanted to marry her, that girl might wonder why."

If Trudi hadn't been there, Theresa would have flung her reason at him there and then, but it wasn't fair to Anita, or to small Inez, to let anyone else know, even old Trudi.

So she said, "Why won't you accept that, Murdoch, that I found I didn't care enough to marry you? With me it's for keeps, marriage."

"Why won't I accept it? Call it intuition if you will. It's not exclusively a woman's quality."

"I think," said Theresa in a voice just as firm, "it's an inability to see yourself as—" She stopped.

"As others see me?"

"As *I* see you. Murdoch, have we got to go on like this? I'm finding it very hard to take. When you spoke to me as you did the day your mother and father were at the Rectory, I accepted your laying-down of rules of conduct . . . ex-fiancées-for-the-use-of. I'd like to lay some down myself now."

"Fair enough. Go ahead."

"I'd like us to call a truce, to act out of school as we act *in* school. Because I can't take much more, presenting a façade of friendliness to the staff, but fighting bitterly, like now, when we meet in private. Let it all be on the surface. Let's stop analysing and probing. Because if not—" She paused and drew in a deep breath.

"If not?"

"If not I'll resign at the end of the year . . . for family reasons."

"Such as?"

She looked across at Trudi and managed a grin. "Trudi and Mother think I'm under the impression that only Brenda was meddling. I knew very well, quite soon, that it was a lot of eyewash. Trudi pretending she was going into a Home in Invercargill! I rang the Home, and they'd never had an application from her. They wanted me home and they knew you had been appointed rector. I think they even consulted Gwenda Lloyd and got her to send that form." She managed a laugh at the look on Trudi's face. "I didn't want to bawl out my poor misguided family because I knew they'd done it from the best of intentions. And perhaps, even apart from you, Murdoch, they thought I'd been away long enough." She laughed again. "Dad saying Mum had lost weight trying to run two homes. Someone blew the gaff on that, she'd been dieting! And it was quite evident nobody knew Trudi had been failing. I'm pretty sure Ngaio caught on that day at the airport and went to the phone to warn you I was coming. So, pet, you can now stop pretending you're feeling so much better now I've come home. And also stop plotting to heal a breach. Tell Mother that too. It just can't be done. But if Murdoch and I hurl bitter things at each other every time we meet in private, I *will* resign. And I love teaching. You're hoist with your own petard, Trudi darling. But if you like to accept the situation as it is, Murdoch, and make things less uncomfortable between your mother and mine, I'll stay for my term of appointment."

Theresa became aware that she wasn't the only one holding her breath for his answer. Trudi was too.

Murdoch said slowly, "Right. No resignation. No more recriminations from now on."

"Goot," said Trudi, rising hastily. She always got a little more Austrian when agitated. "Now, Murdoch, would you be putting the match to the fire in the sitting-room and bring in some logs to fill the big trug, and some coal. Theresa, you can help me get the dinner ready to serve. A goot thing it was in the oven."

Theresa said faintly, "Does he *have* to stay?"

Murdoch grinned, the sort of grin that made the frets and fevers that had been today's portion swing back into the harmonies and simple pleasures of yesterday. "Watch it, that's breaking the cease-fire!"

She grinned back. "Sorry. Perhaps I was wondering how you could possibly eat after all that strudel. And how about Martha?"

"She's gone down to the foot of Wakatipu to her brother's, near Fairlight. I cooked myself a snack for lunch but was still hungry, and even if you don't speak to me all through dinner, I haven't got the strength of will to resist the smell of that sauerbraten. That's what it is, isn't it, Trudi?"

CHAPTER EIGHT

IT SEEMED to Theresa as if time itself slipped back, giving her the sweetness of the days when she had been secure in the knowledge of Murdo's love, when she could dream of a future with him. Here, in this quiet room, they had so often sat with Trudi. This was the place where the adventurous and lawless past and the civilised present-day had met, where the Old World had linked hands with the New.

Either side of the fireplace were the racks of pipes, intricately carved, holding the pipes of all the men of the Klausner family. Theresa liked that touch. Ludwig's were there, Sebastien's, and Grandfather Emil's. Theresa could remember him well as he had sat by the fire, smoking that queer pipe he had brought back from that wedding trip of his to Salzburg, one carved with a lined, nutcracker face, and capped with chased silver. It was his chair Murdoch was sitting in now, also smoking a carved pipe bought in Salzburg. Trudi was opposite him, knitting one of her white cotton bedspreads, and now and then giving him a word he was stumbling over.

Theresa felt a wave of love wash over her, just as it used to do. It wasn't fair that a man's profile could do such things to her. It always had and it seemed as if it always would. Love ought to die when you found your idol had feet of clay, she thought rebelliously.

She returned to her marking, rather surprised that she could give such close attention to it, with him there. True, they had been able to do it years ago. She had liked that, the ability to concentrate on their shared, kindred work.

All of a sudden she burst out laughing, a sound of pure rib-tickling merriment. Trudi and Murdoch looked expectant.

"Oh, this is priceless! One of the rewards of teaching. This makes my week." She looked down at her papers again and chuckled. "Oh, I knew he was starting to take an interest in Robbie Burns, but I never expected anything as good as this. Oh, never. Really, it's a gem. That's what's so marvellous about teaching. Just when you're most despairing, up comes a nugget of pure gold."

"If you don't read it out I shall slit your throat," said Murdoch.

She looked up from it. "Dougal Robertson has had so little interest in English, and none whatever in poetry. He even said to me, "But I think it's just a load of rubbish, Miss Keith." I said, "Well, if that's your opinion, Dougal, I'd appreciate it if you could tell me why it's a load of rubbish. Like in your book reviews. It's not enough just to tell me you don't like a certain book or author. I want to know why."

"He thought for a bit and came up with: 'It's too airy-fairy. Too not-with-it for me.' I tried to draw him out, but it was hard going. 'You mean it's too high-falutin'?' I asked. He reckoned that about described it. I worked out that they'd had just a bit too much Tennyson, Browning, Walter de la Mare earlier. I love them all and so, evidently, did their former teacher. They must have them for sheer beauty of expression, but now and then you get someone — you'll have experienced it time and again, Murdo, I expect — who resents and rejects all, because what they've had doesn't strike a chord in them. I was rather tempted to do a bit of work with him privately, then I felt he might feel he was being got at, forced. So I switched the whole class on to a few more down-to-earth poets — Burns among them, and some very modern ones.

"Since then Dougal's gone mad on Burns and even a few other poets. It's made him a little too aggressively Scots perhaps, considering he was born and bred in New Zealand, as I found the other day. I came across him pummelling Edward Smith because he'd said he liked Shakespeare better than Robbie, and even when I was hauling them apart, Dougal glared at Edward and said, 'What can you expect of a bluidy Sassenach!' But it's done something for him and has opened up his interest in literature, something I'd despaired of. Anyway, I asked the class to write poems based on the style of any poet, favourite or not. I thought it would be a good exercise. This is gorgeous. It's called *A Lament*. Listen:

> The pig 'an I were well acquent,
>   Aye, well acquent were we,
> An' sae I canna bear to tak'
>   A pork chop to ma tea.
> I've scratched his back fu' mony a time
>   An' fed him apple gowks,
> I'll leave the eatin' o' the beast
>   To less warm-herted folks.
> Sae oft we've passed the time o' day
>   Wi' mony a squeal an' grunt,
> His kin were handsome piglets all,
>   An' he the only runt.
> I've loved him long, I've loved him well,
>   He ne'er shall be forgot,
> A thousand curses on the one
>   Who killed him for the pot!
> I'll parritch eat to break ma fast
>   — Nae bacon fried for me,
> Nor tak' till ither pigs be killed
>   A pork chop to ma' tea.

They all chuckled. Nothing like laughter for easing tension. The Rector put out his hand for it. "We must have that in the School magazine at the end of year. He's got right into the spirit of it, hasn't he? You've done a good job there. I don't know that lad yet."

Trudi watched them contentedly as they discussed. This was good. Nothing contentious here. Put enough of this sort of thing into their association and discord could get submerged.

Murdoch said, "Did Fran show you her lists of

things they like, and don't like, that her First Formers produced?"

Theresa shook her head.

Murdoch's expression softened, and he put a hand in his breast pocket inside his jacket. "I got Gwenda to run me off a list. Look."

Their heads bent over it. Murdoch read them aloud for Trudi's sake. "Gwenda put her own comments beside them. As a matter of fact it's so revealing I'd like some educational wallah to see it. Listen: this you could expect because it's from a little fluffy girl. She likes dolls and pretty clothes and roses and coconut ice, and doesn't like spiders, loud noises when it's dark, and liver. But this is from a boy Gwenda describes as a tough hombre very handy with his fists and rather foul-mouthed outside of school. 'Pussy-willow buds all furry, spiderwebs when the dew is heavy on the hedges, waves curling up all green underneath, the wind in our poplar trees, and our cat. He's black and white and he purrs a lot. I don't like semolina, people who aren't kind to animals, and atom bombs.' "

"And Judy Mistoff who is evidently a very stolid unimaginative child is terrified of ghost stories, hates sleeping in the dark, and sewing lessons, loves the rainbows in the waterfalls down Fiordland, the twang of the *tui,* starlings' wings glinting in the sun, and thistledown floating on the wind." He sighed. "I hope life fulfils all their dreams for them. Who knows what's ahead of them? One false step and all that joy in life can be tarnished." He laughed. "Talk about Cassandra-like croakings! Most of them will make out all right, and those little things they like will no doubt compensate them when big things let them down. Nearly finished, Tess? Did you notice there's a documentary on Austria on TV tonight? Put your books away."

Theresa had hoped Trudi would sit between them. Instead Murdoch threw out the cushion there with a true male scorn, stretched his long legs out, and sat

140

down, his shoulders, broad, square, touching Theresa's. She would not allow herself to noticeably draw away. His hand, the one nearest hers, lay on his knee. She had to resist the instinctive urge to put hers over it. Oh, to think that had been her right once. Even a habit.

The first picture cast a spell upon them. The fortress, framed in trees, taken from the path up the Kapuzinerberg, the river at Salzburg, flowing through the town, the crowds gathering in the Platz for the Festival, the Horse Fountain, Mozart's birthplace. Vienna and the Vienna Woods, the Danube, the castle where England's King had once been imprisoned, Tyrolean costumes and music, last of all, Heiligenblut with its bright roofs and gay windowboxes, the village perched on its mountainside above its exquisite valley, the waterfalls, the quivering trees, the slim beauty of the church spire in silhouette against the mountains that might have dwarfed it but only enhanced it. . . .

Then it was over. Trudi sat there, one tear caught in a furrow of her cheek. "So beautiful," she said. "So beautiful, so long ago."

Theresa broke the silence with a banal remark, to break up the trend of her thoughts. Because Heiligenblut had been the place they had promised Trudi years before they would spend their honeymoon in.

"What was the weather like when you went back to Heiligenblut after I left, Murdoch?"

"I didn't go."

"You didn't? I thought you were going with that tour—"

"I changed my mind. When I was there before I found it too—" He stopped.

Theresa very badly wanted him to go on. She said, "Too what, Murdoch?"

He shrugged. "Oh, too perfect. It had been ideal. Nothing to mar it. You know how it is. A mistake sometimes to try to recapture it."

At that moment Brenda burst in, stopped short, took in the scene, said, "Oh, my gosh! Oh, my good gosh!" and gazed at them in enraptured fashion.

Theresa said, "Stop boggling. We've just been watching that TV thing on Austria, that's all. Will you push the couch back now, Murdoch?"

She got up, so did Murdoch, and he complied with her request. He grinned at her little sister. "We've called a truce, Brenda. Nothing more."

Brenda relaxed. "Jolly good idea. Better than all this armed neutrality. *So* immature. I was fed up to the teeth with the two of you, I can tell you."

Theresa said sharply, "Brenda! You ought to remember you're speaking to the Rector of your High School."

Brenda smiled at Murdoch with utmost confidence. "I'm not, am I, Murdo? Not out of school hours. Especially in the bosom of the family. I'm only speaking to my brother-in-law-who-ought-to-have-been!"

"Fair enough, imp. Your sister takes herself far too seriously."

"Don't mind me," said Theresa sarcastically. "Just carry on as if I wasn't here."

He grinned. "Oh, I'd find it hard to completely ignore you. Anyway, Brenda, what brings you here?"

Brenda turned to Trudi. "Grandma, Mother wants to know if that dress fitted Theresa all right. For the Back-to-the-Mining-Days Ball. Because if not she's got a purple delaine one that belonged to Dad's great-grandmother."

Theresa looked surprised. "But I told Trudi I wasn't going to the Ball."

Murdoch barked, "You're not what?"

Theresa said casually, "What a very awkward sentence for a Rector to frame."

He said, "Don't evade. What did you say?"

"I'm not going. That's the weekend I planned to go across-lake to Mahanga-Puke. I met Marie in town one day and it seemed to be the only one she had free of other visitors. It's amazing in a place whose only access is by boat that so many visitors come to stay. They must want to get away from it all."

His tone was brusque. "Of course. But I expect all my staff to be at the Ball. I want it to be a roaring success. It's the kick-off for the Gymnasium Fund."

A flake of colour appeared high on Theresa's cheekbones, a sure sign of temper. "That sounds like a royal command. I find that ridiculous. Mr. Guthrie never insisted. It's not always possible to have one hundred per cent attendance. For instance, Miss Jenner never used to go, she didn't dance."

"But you do. You love dancing."

"I used to. But I'm a newcomer back here and I haven't got a partner. I made this fixture long before the Ball cropped up. It's been a quick decision to have it. We usually have longer notice."

"That couldn't be helped. We can't have too many functions later — what with outside exams and school exams, then the end of year functions. Actually I'm not too keen myself on this being crowded in, but as it's for my pet project, the gym, I didn't feel like damping down all that enthusiasm. With the long holidays coming before too long, it will be almost March before we can get on to anything else. And this will be a super-ball. Can't you go partnerless? You know everybody, you aren't likely to be a wallflower."

He knew darned well she wouldn't have minded going unescorted in this place where she grew up, and besides, her brothers would have filled in, but she hoped he didn't guess it was because she didn't think she could bear to dance in his arms and revive the past as she had done — so briefly — that night at the Doktorwirt.

She said firmly, "Oh, that doesn't come into it. It's the weekend that suits the Campions, and I honestly think one teacher missing won't exactly ruin the Ball."

She saw Brenda raising her eyebrows in a helpless grimace at Murdoch, but decided to ignore it.

Murdoch shrugged and let it go. "I think it's a pity, but I can't insist. Trudi, you'll be on the dowager line, won't you? It gives it local colour. The art master's getting the children busy on huge murals. Jove, we've got some talent there. We want every stress we can get on the cosmopolitan atmosphere of those days. Anita is wearing an old-time Spanish dress. She'll look the part too. Some of the descendants of the Californian miners are going to dress in the costume of the saloon women — plenty of them tailed along, you know. Morag Stuart has a voluminous tartan gown; I'm sure it will look disapprovingly at the lowcut saloon gowns. The Chins and Wongs are coming in their ancestors' outfits, of course, and you're so purely Austrian-looking, Tess, I'd thought you'd have known it would please the Committee."

Theresa decided to drop the subject and turned away a little and was almost sure she saw Brenda mouthing something at Murdoch. Just let her start any of her tricks and see what would happen to her! But she couldn't be a hundred per cent sure.

Trudi began to bustle about, tipping Ferdinand the Golden off her knee in a resentful ball. She'd better get the children some supper or they'd start quarrelling again, was in her mind, they were sure.

She put out sliced currant cake, rich and crumbly, little apple tarts that had a macaroon topping, some squares she called honey-nutties, and cheese and crackers on a board.

Theresa eyed it all and pulled a face as Murdoch drew up his chair with obvious pleasure. "I honestly don't see how you can tuck in again — a cracker will do me. You must have hollow legs."

Brenda looked from one to the other. "You two are friends again!" she said with the delight of one finding a pearl in an oyster.

"Yes, *friends*," said Murdoch with emphasis, "but get this into your head, Brenda Machiavelli Keith, nothing *but* friends."

Theresa told herself later that night, trying to will her chaotic thoughts to sleep, that she was glad of that.

When she got home from playing at the evening service at St. Columba's, Trudi said, "They want you to ring them at Twin Hills."

She put a call through right away. Marie Campion often rang when she felt lonely. The phone was their greatest boon. But it wasn't for a chat. "Tess, I wondered if when you accepted our invitation you knew that was the night of the Parent-Teacher Ball? You must want to go to it, especially as it's an old-timer one. You ought to have said, but I suppose with me saying it was the only weekend within cooee free, you didn't like to put us off. Geoff rode across to Puke-ataahua today, and they told him there. There'll be other weekends later. In fact, we're now thinking of making up a party from the two homesteads here and coming over by launch. The school is so good at including us in such things even if our children are on correspondence and we'd love to give a donation towards the Gymnasium. I can park the children at my sister's. Her youngsters are of an age to be left too, and it gives our governess a change. The shepherds will come too. I do appreciate the fact that you hadn't put us off, but I want to assure you we'd love to come to the dance."

What could Theresa say? Her excuses were dissolving like those mists before the noonday sun. But she wouldn't go unpartnered — in a way — she'd go with the family, as a unit. How truly glamorous!

She didn't think, however, that she could face admitting she was going after all, in front of the staff. So she rang Murdoch. How odd that she could never control the acceleration of her heartbeats when she heard his voice. She must be as nonchalant as possible. "Oh, Rector, I had a ring from Marie Campion. She's keen on coming to the Ball herself, and bringing a party. Yes, the crowd she'll bring will certainly swell the fund. She'd only just heard that it was on that very weekend, so she rang me right away. So I'll be there."

He said quickly, "Tess, about a partner—"

145

"*No*, Murdoch. No. It would just give rise to talk. People would leap to the wrong conclusion. It would be most foolish of you to take me."

His voice was dry. "You've just taken a wrong leap yourself. I was only going to tell you that Robert Armstrong wants a partner. You know Robert — the perfect farmer bachelor, but loves dancing. I was talking to him after morning service. No, I know what you're breaking in to say, I did not suggest it to him. He asked me if any of the new teachers were partnerless. When I suggested you he looked most surprised. He's a very natural, naïve sort of chap, you know, and came out with, 'Why, Murdoch, I thought when I heard Tess was back that you'd made it up.' Then he said my misfortune was his good luck. What about it?"

Theresa made up her mind she must not show chagrin. She was sure he was surprised. She said, "Oh, I'm very fond of Robert. I'd love to go with him. I'll give him a ring. I'd really rather have a partner and he's the most marvellous dancer. As Rector, anyway, you don't need one. By the time you've got all your duty dances in, with all the staff and the wives of the Board and so on, you'll be exhausted."

"Oh, it doesn't apply. I'm taking Anita — Nort asked me. He's got a conference on in Palmerston North that weekend and she was disappointed. Anita thought he had a nerve, but it suits me all right. I'm glad it was okay with the Campions. So long, Theresa."

Theresa reflected that she was showing great control over her temper. She felt justly proud of herself. In actual fact, she would have enjoyed biting a nail in half.

She was determined to get into the Austrian dress that had belonged to her ancestor because the purple delaine would look hideous on her. Purple was such a gorgeous colour, but it didn't suit Theresa at all.

As she came downstairs and walked into the room, Trudi caught her to her. "Oh, my girl, my girl, you are Anna come to life in that, and it makes me want to weep." Trudi brought out from the other room the portrait of Anna, at twenty-two, when she had married Ludwig.

The same brown eyes with the glints of green, the honey-pale hair, the darker brows, a sort of amber colour, the small, exquisitely-shaped ears, the patrician cast of features, the one dimple cleaving the left cheek.

The bodice, tight-fitting above its black lacing, was red and a black silk frill edged the low square neck. The skirt was less than full length and very wide. The rope of jet beads twisted round her throat and falling down to her waist made her fairness stand out even more.

Theresa's father came to pick up Trudi, leaving his daughter to wait for Robert Armstrong. Robert whistled when he came in.

"What luck! I've got the pick of them all!" He whirled her about, began humming a Viennese waltz, and in spite of herself, Theresa felt her feet twitching. Robert was a pet — Murdoch's age. But the girl he should have married had died a month before their wedding, and he'd never met anyone he wanted to put in her place. He wasn't a sad figure, Robert enjoyed life. Nobody would think he was all she could get. Some of them would, no doubt, be prophesying that he had found consolation at last.

The gaiety affected Theresa as soon as she entered the hall. They were a little later than most, because Robert had had a breakdown in the milking machines, and she was glad of it. Robert swung her smartly and expertly into an old-time schottische.

Her eyes, irresistibly, sought for Murdoch in his green swinging kilt. How well men suited that dress, with its jacket a survival of other more gracious days, the lace ruffles, the jewelled pin.

Anita, in his arms, danced with all the grace and abandon of her Spanish ancestry whatever the dance was. Her gown was the purple Theresa longed to wear, with black, and embroidered with sequins. The lace of her mantilla, carefully pinned, framed her ivory cheeks. She looked royal. That was what purple did for you.

It was late in the evening before Murdoch sought Theresa out. She said under her breath, "You don't have to, you know."

He laughed and whirled her out on to the packed floor. "Look a bit obvious if I didn't, wouldn't it? And dancing is dancing no matter whom you're with. We always danced well together. Practice making perfect and all that."

Theresa said, "Anita is the best dancer in the room. She has the fluid grace of her long-ago ancestry, I think."

"I suppose so. But Austrian dancing is so much more fun. It's full of vigour and verve — a sort of romping."

Theresa screwed up her nose. "Doesn't sound as glamorous, though."

"Who cares for glamour?" he retorted, and he looked down into her face, and she found his eyes were serious. Did he mean Rudi? — but *she* meant — they both forgot that eyes could be watching the Rector and his ex-fiancée.

Her look was frank, rather sweet. "Don't most men? They don't always marry glamour, but they like to experiment with it."

"I suppose that's true in some cases. But it wears off, as you found."

She caught her breath. "You'll never believe any other, will you, Murdoch? Well, I'll give up trying to convince you. I've no pride left, in any case. You even had to provide a partner for me."

She thought his arm tightened a little. "Well, perhaps with Rudi it wasn't just glamour. But at least he was — a whole man!"

She twisted back in his arms a little, looked up, trying to read his expression. Their voices were just a thread of sound, pitched under the music in a sort of whispering intensity. Murdoch reversed her expertly, said, "He could ski, climb mountains, do all the things you loved best."

She missed a step, corrected herself, said, "What *can* you mean? You don't mean—?"

"Of course I do. What else? I've always wanted you to come clean, Theresa. Live up to the Keith motto . . . truth conquers. That was what you wanted, wasn't it, Tess, someone who could do all those things?"

She made a slight sound, but checked.

He said, "I became lame, Theresa. Oh, long before I proposed to you. I've always wondered if you just thought you owed it to me seeing that in a way, it was in rescuing you. Then you found you couldn't take it, that those things meant more to you. Skiing was quite beyond me. It must have irked you being tied to a lame man in the snow sports season. I couldn't attempt those long climbs we'd known. It was bound to react on you — a child of the mountains. So restricting. It aged me too. Rudi was so young, exactly your age, and his skill on skis was known in two hemispheres. I thought my days on the mountainsides were over. Then that surgeon patched me up. But it made no difference. You didn't even notice I wasn't limping that day on the Kapuzinerberg."

Fury filled Theresa to overflowing. She said, keeping perfect time, because when she and Murdoch danced they were as one, but she said it through her teeth, "You thought that of me! That I couldn't take your lameness? Thank you for the compliment. My goodness, now I do believe I had a lucky escape. I thought you understood me so well. But you don't even begin to know me!" She gave a strange laugh, almost slightly hysterical, though low. "How useless then it was, all those years. Those early years. Oh, it has its funny side, it really has. You thought I gave you up for that? Murdoch, I've never conquered my fear of skiing. I only ever went skiing because of you. I wanted to share your enthusiasms. That's why I was happier for you, that day on the Kapuzinerberg, about your cricket. Do you know something? After we parted, I never went skiing again. Not once in Austria, despite all Rudi did to make me. It doesn't matter now if I say I'd wanted to come on down the Macetown Track hours before, that day. It was Geraldine's wilfulness led us into danger. It wasn't that, Murdoch. It was another flaw in your character that made me doubt you, made me wonder were you the sort of man I wanted to father my children. Oh, it's so funny to think you thought that of me. Murdoch, this dance is nearly over. I think I'll go to the powder-room. Don't come near me the rest of the night, please — I just couldn't bear it. By Monday morning I'll have cooled off. Oh, why, oh, why did my family conspire to bring me home? I could have been still in Salzburg."

The rest of the evening Theresa spent in wild gaiety. She owed it to Robert, who was sweet, to look as if she enjoyed every moment. But it was a pity he took her home past Anita's cottage. The Rector's American car he had shipped back to New Zealand from Canada was at the gate.

As they passed Theresa looked through the trees to the house. It was a blaze of lights, there on its rise. The curtains were not drawn in the sitting-room. Theresa caught a glimpse of rich purple, another of a blue-green kilted figure. Perhaps Anita would cook Murdoch bacon-and-eggs. Some of the others were finishing off with that. Some of the staff. She'd heard Murdoch ask Anita if she would like to join in.

She had said no, she must go home. So the Rector had gone with her, naturally enough. But he hadn't just dropped her at the gate. And Nort was away up in the North Island.

Theresa felt deathly tired. She thanked Robert, and went straight to bed.

CHAPTER NINE

LIFE at Kotare High School went on just the same. No one could have detected any change in Theresa's attitude to her Principal or in his to her. But although she herself had terminated their dealings the night of the Ball, she felt intensely irritated by the fact he did not seek her out to discuss it further. That, she knew, was completely irrational on her part.

She knew why she wanted the subject to come up again, however. Because when it did, she was going to tell him exactly why she had given him up. Geraldine had had no right to exact that promise from her. And her advice had been all wrong too, to invent other reasons for giving him up. But Murdoch didn't come to her. And she couldn't quite bring herself to seek him out for it.

The everyday routine made it difficult for her to nurse the sense of injury she had over the fact he'd thought she had given him up because of his lameness. Routine lulled you and there were times when she felt very sympathetic to him and sorry for the things a Principal got involved in whether he liked it or not. Outwardly, when he had to deal with instances of gross misbehaviour or complicated family situations that were affecting children's conduct or progress at school, he was very much the master of the situation. Inwardly, Theresa knew, there must be times when his very soul would shrink from interfering. But then every Rector worth his salt took some things to heart, adding lines round his mouth, carving one between his brows.

Theresa was looking forward to the weekend across-lake at Twin Hills. Marie and Geoffrey were such kindred spirits and there was such a welter of things to do . . . seasonal work on the big sheep-station, riding, playing tennis, experimenting with a little white ball on the nine-hole golf-course on the property, helping Marie with household tasks. That homestead had the best private library in the Lake District, so even wet weather was no bogey, and the house could have been dubbed: Hobbies Unlimited.

It was the last break before the School Certificate examinations, so it was very welcome. Theresa wished she could have had these children all year. It wasn't good for them to have a change of teacher during that important year, but she'd tried to make up for that and thought she'd have a moderate number of successes.

Geoffrey was coming across for her, in their private launch. Theresa closed her mind to the memory of the weekend she and Murdoch had once spent there, shortly after their engagement. They had climbed up Big Twin one night, when the moon had been high over the lake and the whole world had been a magic one.

Oh, well, it promised to be an idyllic weekend. The spirits of the staff as well as the children rose. Almost all the teachers were going away somewhere. Some to the cities where their people lived, to relax in a home atmosphere; some were joining a party for the Routeburn Track, travelling up-lake by boat towards the Head of Wakatipu, then shouldering their packs and cutting deep into the back country.

Murdoch and Mike were going across Moana-kotare, but not to Twin Hills. They would be landed in a remote inlet of river and would take a seldom-used track deep into the bush and mountains, using a deerstalkers' hut as base. This was to be almost a surveying jaunt, because there was some talk of this track being improved and used as part of an adventure course for Otago schoolboys, and Murdoch wanted to do a survey of his own to form an advance opinion of the suitability and safety of the terrain.

Murdoch and Mike were both extremely well versed in such things and knew similar tracks in the Queenstown area very well. They had good maps, compasses, equipment. And, reflected Theresa, rather despising herself for worrying, at least they weren't hunting, so there'd be no danger from firearms.

She was determined to enjoy this weekend to the full. Imagine three full days. She'd done enough prep the week before to free her for the full time.

When she got down to the jetty, in plenty of time so as not to hold Geoffrey up when he came for her, the launch Mike and Murdoch had engaged to take them across to Tiki Point was being loaded up with their gear, and she turned her head to see the two men carrying some more across from Murdoch's car.

They looked so happy and carefree in their tramping outfits. No wonder. A whole long weekend free of school cares, no pupil problems, no parent problems, no ex-fiancées to quarrel with!

Murdoch put up a hand to shade his eyes against the brilliance of the morning sun. "I think I see Geoff coming across now, Theresa. You'll have a great weekend there. Isn't it the most marvellous morning? I can really believe summer is almost here. Not a shred of mist on the Remarkables, see . . . we won't have to wait for noon today for full sun."

The sun glinted, diamond-bright, on the white spray of the triangle of wake Geoffrey's launch was making and it was coming too swiftly for Theresa. It was too stupid of her. She wanted to ask Murdoch not to go. Plain mad. It wasn't a premonition, so don't be silly! She didn't believe in such things. She hadn't much patience with people who vowed they'd felt a coming disaster in their bones. It was nearly always hindsight, not foresight.

It's sheer envy, you foolish girl. You want to be doing this trip with him, just as you did many shorter trips with him all those years ago. You want to be married to him, as you ought to have been by now, setting off with a pup-tent in case of being held up in the forest-lands, planning the fun of spending a couple of nights in that deerstalkers' hut they were talking about.

Geoffrey came in, his two eldest children with him, Astrid, a tall fair twelve-year-old, and Richie, dark and stocky, ten. Theresa got on board. Then in that split second between saying a nonchalant goodbye to the two men on the wharf, and moving off words were jerked out of her again. She turned back suddenly, the thick creamy swirl of hair flying out, and she heard her own voice saying, "Take care, won't you, Murdo? It's wild country."

Murdoch grinned instantly and said, "Once more, Grandmamma, thank you. We will." Again Theresa had to avoid a knowing pair of eyes — this time, Mike's.

Well, just as well these embarrassments she brought upon herself were always at the point of goodbye. They didn't last. Geoffrey set his course for Mahanga-puke and Theresa would not allow herself to took back.

She got a great welcome from Marie, down at the homestead jetty. What a glorious place it was, completely self-contained. The storehouses were always stocked like grocery shops, the medicine chest an enormous one, with up-to-date drugs and other supplies, and as much of the more perishable stuff as possible produced on the station or stored in the deep-freeze units. They could have withstood a siege of several months.

Back up at the homestead, consuming with reckless disregard for calories, vast amounts of fresh pikelets, scones, biscuits and coffee, Theresa said, "It's so good of you to have me this weekend, Marie. I know you're still terrifically busy." Twin Hills was a high-country station, so they didn't begin lambing till the end of the first week in October and were still constantly riding round the sheep, either on horseback, or by Land-Rover, matching motherless lambs with lambless ewes, filling bottles, resuscitating weak ones. But the weather was in their favour just now.

"It's been almost too good for the time of year. I hope we aren't building up to some spectacular storm. It's the oddest thing, isn't it, how Labour Weekend always has such a bad reputation, according to statistics, for rain? It will be just marvellous having you, Tess. I sent the governess off for the weekend, and

Geoff let one of the shepherds go — his sister is getting married in Invercargill. You'll be able to help with the lambs and keep an eye on the children too. But I had a real onslaught on things this week, and I aim to spend as much time as possible outside with you. Have the sort of meals where I bung everything in the oven and come back to find it cooked. Praise the Lord for who ever invented casseroles. The tins are full to the brim too. Sylvie — the governess — was sport enough to offer to help me with that chore. She's a gem. But tell me, any further word of this five-day hostel being built for Kotare?"

Marie was so sensible, so affectionate, so unchanging. She said as they washed the morning-tea dishes and put the casserole in, "I'm going to put your mind at rest about one thing, Theresa. I'm not going to talk about your broken engagement this weekend. Apart from thinking it's your business and no one else's, I'm terribly fond of you both. I went to school with Murdoch, as you know, and I admire him greatly, and I boarded with your grandmamma for four years when there was no school bus from our valley, so I knew you from a tiny child, and I love you too. Anita told me she'd had a try at healing the breach but felt she'd done nothing — I thought then you might have been doubtful about coming over here, that I might have a go. I wouldn't dream of it. Matchmakers only succeed in stirring up the mud sometimes."

Theresa leaned forward and dropped a kiss on Marie's cheek. There was real gratitude in her tone. "Oh, thank you. Now I can really enjoy my weekend. I'd feel so much freer to come and go here — at such times you can collect me — if I knew you wouldn't be contriving ways to get Murdoch over here at the same time." She added, "As a matter of fact, he's on this side of the lake, with Mike Channing, plotting out the area for this Otago Adventure project."

"Oh, up the Tawhiti Valley? Geoff was telling me. They thought they would establish a chain of huts. Ideal, I'd say. Even the name. Doesn't it mean far away? The Far Away Valley Camp. I must suggest it."

The weekend sped on wings, yet Theresa felt it had put a welcome stretch of time between the problems she had faced when she first came home, and the rest of the term. By January Catriona McCorkill would be in New Zealand. Murdoch had said the other day that he'd heard of a vacancy coming up at the Queenstown High School and had advised her to apply, though there was no knowing if she'd get it or not.

Fortunately it had been in the staffroom in general conversation, so it hadn't fallen to Theresa to answer.

Frances had. "Is she keen on teaching in this area?"

"Yes. Natural enough. It's so scenic and she's heard so much about it. She has relations in Oamaru, though, so failing getting a position here, she may try there. Not too far away."

Not too far from the scenery? Or from one Murdoch Gunn?

Theresa went to bed on the Sunday night knowing regret that tomorrow would be her last day and that in the spring twilight Geoffrey would ferry her over the lake, pick up the governess and the shepherd, and she'd plunge into the strenuous work of the end of the year.

It was four in the morning when the spectacular electrical storm woke everyone in the house. In all the years Theresa had spent among the mountains, she had never heard anything like it.

It must have been centred clean over the homestead . . . they all woke at the same moment, and, as they later found, comparing reactions, had cowered in their beds, not knowing in that first confused moment, summoned from sleep in such a shattering manner, what had happened. It sounded as if the very heavens had been riven, as if the mountainsides above the homestead had been split from top to bottom . . . what was it, an earthquake? There seemed to be continuing reverberations.

She heard the children rushing helter-skelter to their parents' bedroom. The next violent crash sent Theresa running for the same place. She was in the tail, but was in time to see Astrid hurl herself on to her parents' bed, scrabble to get between them. She was white to her lips, and she sort of gibbered, "It's a—a—a c-cataclysm!" Richie, diving after her, yelled "It's an earthquake, a landslide—oh, Dad!"

"It's all right!" said Geoffrey. "It—it's only a thunderclap," but he didn't look really convinced.

Astrid's voice squeaked. "It *couldn't* be only thunder. I thought it was shaking the house apart."

Richie said, "It—it couldn't be an explosion, could it?"

Theresa looked round, saw Marie's dressing-gown, caught it up, pulled it round her, sat down on a stool. "I'm as scared as the kids. What could it have been?"

The dogs had set up the most eerie howling. The clamour, in the stillness that had succeeded the cataclysmic sound, raised prickles along their spines. Almost a sound of doom.

Geoffrey sprang out of bed, rushed to the window, pulled back the blue and purple curtains. "The men are all awake. Their lights are on. It must have sounded appalling over their small huts. Tin roofs too!" At that moment a white blinding light seared and split the whole sky over Little Twin, a light so fierce it actually paled the elecric light inside the room.

"Come away from that window, Geoff," commanded Marie, "You might get struck."

"The men are coming," said Geoffrey, "charging down the hillside at the rate of knots. I think they've probably decided their huts will never stand the force of the deluge we're going to get. They'll leak all over the place. But they'll be lucky if they make it."

They didn't. The skies opened and the water poured out in a solid mass, it seemed. The doors at Twin Hills were never locked. They all rushed to swing them open, however, and men fled in, their pyjamas plastered to them.

"Into the showers in the laundry," ordered Geoffrey. "I'll rustle up some clothes for you. It's too fierce to last, I think, but we'll have to be prepared for anything. Not that we'll be able to see the damage till daylight. That lightning must have brought trees down. Hope they don't block the creeks, that's all. Every gully will be up in any case and I think we'll have leaks even in this house. No guttering could carry away this volume of water."

The children were recovering now and beginning to enjoy themselves. "Bet nobody else got it as bad," said Richie. "It was right over our place."

"A wider area than that, son, I'd say," said his father. "A very large storm-centre, and right over this side of the lake. Fancy it happening Labour Weekend. I hope there are no tragedies. There are bound to be parties of campers and trampers. Even the experienced ones would find this tough. As long as they keep to high ground it wouldn't be so bad, but every river's going to be up to danger level in an hour or less. It was so close to the watersheds. Oh—"

He had seen Marie's warning gesture too late. He turned to Theresa who had lost her colour again. "Murdoch'll be okay, Tess. He's too old a backwoodsman to take risks. He and Mike will be in that deer-stalkers' hut and it's built for bad weather. They may get holed up for a bit, that's all. He'll make Mike wait before they attempt any river crossings. It's the younger foolhardy ones I worry over."

But for Theresa it felt as if an enormous weight had come down on her, constricting her heart, her breathing, her pulses. Murdoch was out in that shrieking compound of elements that seemed bent on destruction and fury, hurling unleashed hatred and force against a cowering, helpless world.

The noise continued in frightening, staccato periods, the rain poured down after each cloud was rent. The men, reappearing in Geoff's farm-clothes, began to bring out oil lamps, set them round the rooms. They were used to power failures here, though it was usually winter when the weight of snow brought the lines down.

At that moment the rain stopped completely. The

silence was almost too oppressive. They felt they were waiting for another hideous outburst. It did come, but it had been a longer spell and in thankfulness they could hear the water from the roofs pouring away. They crowded out on to the concrete-floored porch when it started again. It was magnificent to watch if they hadn't known what disasters it would bring in its wake to stock, to buildings and pastures . . . and to men, caught out there, in these pitiless elements. Theresa, against her will, could think of nothing but that premonitory feeling that had swept over her when she'd said good-bye to Murdoch on Saturday morning on the sunlit shore.

The phone rang. Geoff took it — the Mayor of Ludwigtown. "Are you all right? Worst storm in my generation, I'd say. You are? Thought I'd better ring before communication goes. It's bound to go, I'm afraid. Use the radio transmitter if it does and you get news of any trampers needing help. Or if we get news from other quarters, and you're nearer, we'll be in touch. The Rector is over there, with the woodwork master, in the Awhitu, but they'll be in the deerstalkers' hut. It's very sturdy and high up. There are some hunters further in, due out today, but they may have gone to the hut by now. I'm afraid there are a devil of a lot around Wakatipu and Mount Aspiring National Park, but though it will be bad, I think it was your side that copped the worst. It seemed to be centred right over you." They talked on for a short time, making arrangements for transmitting, and even before they had finished the lights had gone. A quarter of an hour later the phone was dead. They were as isolated as ever they had been in the old days.

Before daybreak the rain had ceased, but it had been a phenomenal fall and when the watery dawn came up, it was a scene of desolation, all its beauty drowned and limp. It was battered, saturated, frightening.

Maria and Theresa filled the men up with hot food and they set out to rescue stock, though on a high country run such as this, the animals would instinctively

159

scramble to higher places. Not like out on the flat where whole paddocks would be submerged.

A watery sun came through and began to light up the grey murky waters of the lake, strewn with debris and occasionally the grim humps of carcases, sheep, cattle, the occasional deer even. Impossible to believe that yesterday these same waters had been so blue and so clear that at the edge one could see the shingle glinting in the sunlight. Now, where only dry creek-beds had existed, a hundred torrents were pouring mud and clay into the trough of the lake. The driest spring on record had ended dramatically.

Cold fear kept Theresa's heart in its tight tentacles. They had the radio going incessantly for news. She kept going up to the lookout tower to use the strong binoculars there. Yesterday, when it didn't matter, Geoffrey had vowed he'd seen a plume of smoke beyond the Awhitu hills, probably from the hut. But today the atmosphere was so thick and sullen, nothing could be seen, and their only hope was that fitful sun. It might clear.

Suddenly, dramatically, the clouds rolled away from the hills, a little more warmth came into the sun, and the visibility widened. Lovely to see that steely horizon retreating.

Theresa ran up the stairs again. She picked up the binoculars, focused them uplake. Suddenly she saw something. That is, if she wasn't imagining it. Nobody *rowed* down this lake! It was too vast, even if Wakatipu dwarfed it. She focused again. But somebody *was* rowing. And from the direction of the Awhitu!

She ran down, calling out. Geoff had just come in and sprang for the stairs, mud and all, great chunks of it falling off him. He confirmed it. The others crowded round, impatiently snatching at the glasses. No hope of telling who it was. They could just make out the motions of rowing, rhythmic, desperate rowing.

Theresa's voice croaked, "It's from up there—where he is." He. Only one person in her mind. She realised it with shame, said, "Oh, if only they're both all right!"

160

"Steady," said Geoffrey. "It might be neither. Don't let's fear the worst. There was that old rowing-boat up there. They used to use it for crossing that tiny lake — the *Dewdrop*. Come on, boys. He must be nearly all in. Come and help me with the launch, we'll meet him."

Marie had raced downstairs ahead of them, thrust a small flask of brandy at them. In no time they were away, shooting out into the lake waters with a speed that must have seemed miraculous to that lone, gallant rower.

Theresa stood beside Geoffrey, straining her eyes. Prayers were often selfish at such times, but it rose from her heart involuntarily, "Let it be Murdo, let it be Murdo."

There came the moment when she knew it wasn't; another when she recognised Mike. As he saw they were near, he stopped rowing, and leaned forward in utter exhaustion. *He'd made it!*

They slowed down, came about, then alongside.

Mike looked up. Theresa was surprised to find her voice obeying her will. "Mike . . . where's Murdoch? Is he—"

He could hardly frame the words, his mouth was so dry. "Yes—so far. Gone to rescue a chap stranded on the island in the Awa-awhiowhio. Mightn't be an island very long. Got to get help. Got to get help fast."

"Help's here," said Geoffrey. "Mike, we're going to tow you. But here's a flask . . . take a swig of that." Then, "Can you tie the tow-line or are your hands frozen?"

"I'll manage."

Theresa's mind was giving house-room to one phrase only, and it was beating against the walls of it. The island in the Awa-awhiowhio . . . the island that sometimes didn't exist, but built up again when the floods that had swept it away had subsided, and the river-boulders, tumbled down from the heights by the waters, settled again. The Awa-awhiowhio. She wished she she didn't know the meaning of the name. The River of the Whirlpool. The only way to the land at this side was across that evil pool. The other side was bordered by sheer cliffs where the river had cut away the rock in aeons long past. Some strange combination of eddy and contour forced the stream up against the island and swirled right round on itself except when the river was very low.

They came up to the jetty where Marie and the children were waiting with blankets, hotwater bottles, hot coffee, just in case. She took one look at Mike's grey face, then his raw hands, and held the cup to his lips.

He took only a few mouthfuls, but gratefully, then said, "Two deerstalkers. One reached our hut, said his friend had been swept down river, sucked into the whirlpool, and flung up on the island. But he was alive —had actually raised himself up and gestured to his friend. He was all in himself. Had gashed himself badly on submerged barbed wire. He's lost a lot of blood but he's okay. Murdoch went off to see what he could do about helping this chap. It was about eight this morning."

What would Murdoch do? Would he simply go to the bank this side, keeping watch, calling encouragement to the boy, telling help was near, that a 'copter would come in? He would gauge every eroding inch, standing by till the very last. Or—but it was impossible. When he had done it he'd been in his twenties, strong as an ox, and long before he had injured his leg muscles. But Theresa knew the answer. Murdoch would attempt anything rather than see a lad swept to his death as that clay and rock island disintegrated.

Action was swift. Geoff raced up to the house to see if Phil had the transmitter working. He had. He barked out instructions, the locality. "If the island's not gone, the helicopter is that lad's only hope. If it has, then — it's over."

Marie had the first-aid kits in the launch, provisions, blankets, folding-stretchers. Neither she nor Geoff forbade Theresa to go. She was a child of the mountains, sure-footed as a goat, thanks to her unwilling experiences with Murdoch, long ago, slim but tough, and Phil must stay with the transmitter in case it broke down again, and they could need two stretchers, so four bearers.

Theresa thrust her feet into tramping boots. Geoff made terrific speed up-lake, but never sacrificed safety to it, for the debris in the lake was the worst they had ever seen.

Action seemed suspended in Theresa till the inlet came in sight. Never had they tied up so quickly, or so securely. They worked with the efficiency of desperation. The short cut was in itself hazardous, with the whole surface greasy yellow clay, but they put Theresa between them, and her footing was as sure as the men's.

Theresa wanted to hold time still, that remorseless fragment of eternity that could make all the difference to life itself for those two men, in the final wearing-away of that island. She looked up as Geoff said, "Another five minutes and we'll be able to see the river-bed."

She thought, *"Five minutes . . . and everything I hold most dear could be swept away out of that cutting, swirled helplessly with crumbling rocks and churning uprooted trees, right down the short stretch of river into the bottomless lake!"*

Oh, she knew now, when it might be too late, that Anita didn't matter. Nothing mattered, except that Murdoch should be safe.

They came to the crest of the ridge, Geoff in the lead. He stopped dead, and in his stillness Theresa knew the answer, even before her legs somehow carried her on to stand beside him. She stood as if turned to stone.

Below them was an unbroken stretch of water, yellow, evil, boiling like a cauldron, from bank to bank. Slowly, painfully, she turned her head as if her neck would scarcely obey the instructions from her brain, and saw down below huge trunks of trees being tossed about like corks before the current finally swirled them towards the bend round which the river entered the lake.

The other two reached them, stood in silence. Then one of them said roughly, "We've got to search. Miracles *do* happen. They may have been flung up. Come *on!*" They began to scramble down to the edge, or what remained of it. But Theresa knew the search could only be for bodies. Now she prayed they might find them, take them back, give them fitting burial. She didn't want the lake to hold them for ever.

Geoff held her hand tightly. She freed it by force. "No," she said fiercely, "we go quicker alone." It was true. Sympathy must wait.

She would never forget the half-hour that followed. There were very few shingle banks left, though huge logs had been tossed up on to those narrow strips that remained. So they must search them well. They could not go round the bend to see the mouth and the lake. The waters had scoured away all the river-beach there, but there was a natural track winding up among the battered beeches there, made, no doubt, by deer.

Theresa was no longer aware of the painful drawing in of her breath that had hampered her before, or of the scratches on her hands as she hauled herself up by scrub and tussock and branch. She just went on and on. When they came to the top, and went to the edge, they would look over, and if the beach below this bluff was empty of human trace, she would know it was all over.

They all hesitated, looked at each other, made to move on to the edge. Then it happened. By the great beech, over the edge of the narrow track a head appeared. No, two heads, because the first belonged to one man, crawling, the other, further back, to someone he was carrying slumped on his back.

The first head was down, looking at the ground, just inches from his face, looking as if nothing else mattered to him but progress inch by inch. The second one was lolling sideways. *But the first belonged to Murdoch.* And he was alive, if only just.

They all managed to choke back their cry of incredible joy, because he wasn't — quite — over the edge, and he might slip back from fright. They held their breath as he edged on a foot or two from the brim, a great shuddering sob was torn from him, and he lifted his head a little, said, "Then Mike made it!" and passed out on them.

Weariness fell from the four of them like a snake sloughing off a skin. They sprang at those two figures.

Geoff said, "Take the top one gently. I don't like the look of that leg."

It was obviously broken. Oh, how marvellous these high-country men were, especially those who lived across the lake, with no speedy access to doctors and hospitals. They splinted the leg. Plenty of wood littered the ground, so they could be selective. They must make it immobile till it could be set expertly.

They fitted the stretchers together, working swiftly, while Geoff and Theresa tried to minister to the two men, both unconscious now. "They've been out of the water some time," said Geoff. "I reckon Murdoch must have managed to get the water out of the boy. Perhaps he passed out himself then, recovered and then dragged him up. He wouldn't dare try to splint the leg, I suppose, in case what beach had been left disappeared. But we'll find out when they come round. Just as well they're still out to it. Easier on them. We'll have to take them the long way round. We'd never get down that track."

It was a nightmare trip, but nothing mattered really, save that they still lived. They would get them to civilisation and expert aid somehow.

They made the hut, found the other deerstalker recovering. He was weak, but mobile, and at the moment of their entry was preparing to go in search of Murdoch and his mate. They thought none the worse of him because he cried when he saw the two men were, at least, alive.

They decided, after a rest, to continue down to the launch, and straight across-lake to the Ludwigtown Hospital. The men showed no signs of revival all the hideous way down to the launch. It seemed the acme of comfort, even if it was crowded now. It took them three-quarters of an hour to cross the water and they were thankful the storm was spent, and the waters still, with debris the only hazard.

Theresa knelt beside Murdoch, holding his hands, touching his face, her eyes never leaving it. If only before she had to deliver him into the care of others, he would open his eyes, recognise her, if he could know he had saved the boy!

There were people on the jetty when they got there, residents ruefully inspecting the damage the storm had done to their lake-front, with whole trees uprooted, and shingle flung up across the esplanade. Not many people because it was the time of the evening meal, but they went into instant action. An estate car appeared as if by magic, and the stretchers were lifted into it. Theresa and Geoff scrambled in beside them, crouching on the floor, holding them still. The injured friend of the rescued boy was helped in beside the driver and slowly they came to the cottage hospital, which was a blaze of lights.

Theresa had the greatest confidence in Doctor Riesdahl. Experience was what counted here. He had been born amongst these mountains and the situations he had coped with in getting to injured mountaineers, before helicopters solved so many difficulties, had made him a mountaineer himself.

Both men were, of course, suffering from exposure. The leg was set, plastered. The boy showed signs of returning to consciousness. His friend had his wounds cleaned, stitched, an injection against tetanus given. It seemed as if Murdoch was suffering from delayed concussion. He had two nasty wounds on his head, probably from trees hurtling down the river. The Sister brought them all hot drinks, arranged for her small staff to assist them to hot baths, managed to provide a change of clothing, anointed their scratches and bruises.

The Sister said to Theresa, "Would you like to stay beside him, Tess? The cook told me his people had

166

intended being up here this weekend, but their married daughter sent word she was coming to Dunedin to see them, so they stayed home. So he has no one here, and you—"

Theresa was glad the Sister just accepted the fact that she was nearest to Murdoch. They had such a small staff they were glad of her help. She made the last cups of tea, washed up the dishes, while they made their patients comfortable for the night. It gave her something to do.

Then she settled by Murdoch's bed. The night nurse whispered to her, "Call me the moment there's any change in him. I'll be in and out constantly, of course. He may come round soon. It may be later."

Theresa was conscious of an immense and frustrating helplessness. To do nothing but wait was well-nigh intolerable. Slowly the hands of the ward clock went round.

She heard a noise and expected it to be the nurse. It was her mother. Elisabeth's face was drawn and full of pity.

Elisabeth said, "I've brought you my blue cloak. You get so cold sitting still, I *know*."

She knew! It swept over Theresa then, how often mothers sat by bedsides, counting the hours, praying, steeling themselves to accept the fact that loved ones are not immortal, but doing all that was humanly possible, to keep the spark of life flickering.

She stood up and Elisabeth slipped the blue cloak around her, pulled the hood up over her head, its edging of white fur framing Theresa's face. "It keeps all draughts out, too."

Theresa sat down again, respossessed herself of Murdoch's hand. Her mother's eyes fell to the two hands.

Theresa said desolately, "He can't feel it, though." Murdoch had gone away from her into a land where she could not follow. Where he was aware of nothing, not even pain.

Elisabeth said softly, "I'm sure Murdoch will be

helped by this. Long before he has the strength to speak to you he'll know your hand is in his and that you love him."

She said these last words in a very matter-of-fact tone, but Theresa was startled by them. She turned her face, in its hood, towards her mother, questioning in her eyes.

Elisabeth said, "Don't deny it, *Liebling,* not in a moment like this. I've known ever since you came back that you still love him."

Theresa said, "All right. I always have. There were other reasons why I wouldn't marry him — big reasons. But none of them matter now. I was looking for something too ideal, I couldn't bear to settle for less. But in any case, Murdoch won't love me now. Not the way I've—"

There was the suggestion of a smile in Elisabeth's whispering. "Well, I can only guarantee it up till last Thursday, of course, but that ought to be recent enough for you."

"Thursday! But, Mother—"

"He dropped in when you were at Queenstown after school and found me alone for once. We had a long chat. He asked me if marriages worked when one person loved the other much more than he was loved in turn. I had to say I didn't know. It was possible. But why? He said he loved you as much as ever, and he'd done everything possible to rouse you but couldn't. He'd even tried to make you jealous of that Canadian girl, seeing that had worked with Rudi and Lisa. But it had been no go. Catriona isn't coming to New Zealand alone, he tells me. She has a young man back home who's coming here too, for a working holiday.

"Listen, dear. Whatever it was that made you break that engagement, you must tell Murdoch the real reason. When he's better. If you can tell me, later, well and good. If not, all right. You mustn't go back into your shell again. Now I'm going back into the night nurses' room, I'll be there to relieve you if you want a break, or get sleepy. But I'd like to leave you alone with him now."

Theresa held up her face for her mother's kiss. "I will tell him, Mother. Tell him why, and he will understand, and sort it out for me. Some day I hope I can tell you and Trudi too, but no one else, ever."

It was half-past three, that horrible hour when human vitality is at its lowest, and hope seems something that belongs only to daylight. What Elisabeth had told her had comforted Theresa, but through it all was the pain of knowing it just might be too late.

But it was then that the fingers in hers suddenly moved, trying to turn themselves over, trying to grasp hers, but very feebly. She leaned forward, her honey-coloured locks swinging out under the blue hood. "Murdo? Murdo? Can you hear me, Murdo? I'm here — Theresa!"

His eyelids flickered a little, then lay still again as if weighted down. Her voice now was only a thin thread of sound, "Murdo . . . Murdo?"

The lids flickered again, the eyes opened finally, looked vacant, unrecognising, staring straight ahead, but then, at the sound of her voice saying his name over and over, they turned, and with difficulty focused.

It was the merest hint of a smile, a faint widening of the lips, the flicker of a light in the dark eyes. He said, "Tess . . . ?"

She nodded. He tried to frame some more words, gave up, then, moistening his lips, managed, "Did I— keep hold of him? Did I get him—to shore?"

Theresa said, "You not only got him to shore. You crawled up the bluff with him on your back. Don't you remember that bit?"

"No. Will he—live?"

"He's in better shape than you are. Murdo, I must get the nurse. Those are my orders. As soon as you came round I was—"

The fingers tightened quickly. "Not yet, Tess. Got something to ask you."

She waited. It seemed a long time. Would he speak again?

The lids lifted and once more there was the hint of a smile. And something else? What? Confidence?

Yes, that must have been it, because he said, "You do love me, don't you Theresa?"

"Yes, Murdo, I love you. I always have."

A suggestion of a frown. "Then why—?"

She said swiftly, "Murdo, darling, I must get the nurse, I'm not to excite you. I'll tell you why when you're better. Not now, my love."

He said, "It's the first time I've not had the ring on me. Couldn't take it on a trip like that. Might've lost it. It's in my desk at the Rectory. Wear it when you come to see me later today, Tess. Promise?"

"I promise, Murdo. I must tell them you're conscious."

He slowly relinquished her hand. "You look like that picture of the Blue Madonna in that. I like it. Tell Mother I'll be all right."

The nurse came, the poor overworked doctor was back for another confinement. "I'm sure the thunder does it," he grumbled. "They say it addles eggs under hens, so why not promote labour pains? It's an interesting theory. But I'm glad I was here."

Theresa left them to it, went to her mother. When they returned they told them Murdo had lapsed before they had quite finished, but it had been very helpful to have him conscious when they examined him.

The doctor went back to his other patient. Came back to say things were going well, and he could spare Theresa a few moments.

Elisabeth knew him so well. After all, he had delivered Theresa and her other three children. She caught on, said, "Would you like me to leave the room, Doctor?"

He nodded. He said to Theresa when the door closed, "Not long now till daylight. You can stay till breakfast-time and ring his parents then, but tell them not to come here."

Theresa caught her breath in. "But Murdo? Are there complications? It's serious? Those head injuries — do you fear a fractured skull? Is—"

"Hang on, lass! We'll have X-rays taken, of course, now he's a bit rested, but that's not it. That leg injury of his was an unusual one. But there's something not quite right there at the moment. I'll want you to tell Hetty and James that there are no serious injuries apparent, but not to start up here because I may have him transferred to Dunedin. Say I'll ring them when I've finalised that, they can meet him at Momona and his mother can travel with him to hospital in the road-ambulance. But nothing's definite yet. Don't say too much about the unconsciousness. He may lapse from time to time. Say he gets periodic concussion. Not to worry. Look, I've changed my mind about you staying till daylight. You look all in."

She bit her lip. "Doctor, what if I told you that during the night when he first recovered consciousness, he asked me to resume the engagement and I promised I would?"

At the look on his face she said quickly, "I tried to stop him talking, truly. I said I'd been told to get the nurse the moment he opened his eyes. But he wouldn't let me go till he asked me. I thought you were supposed to humour a patient, not argue with him."

The stern face mellowed. "All right. Look — no time now, we must get this straightened out some time. Perhaps even an old medico can help in this realm too. But I can't risk having him excited any more, happily or otherwise. If you've promised him that, his mind will be at rest. He's got a marvellous constitution and he'll probably be okay, and even if it has started off the old trouble with his leg again, he managed with a limp before. Now off. I'll let you know when to ring his parents about times."

When she did, it was to tell them that the doctor had by now ascertained that the surgeon who had done such wonders on Murdoch's leg was now at Dunedin, and Murdoch would be under his care.

When Theresa put the phone down she said crisply, "I'm going to school. I can't sit home twiddling my thumbs, and can't very well keep ringing the Dunedin Hospital. And we're one short as it is, this week. Miss Symons wasn't to be back till next Monday."

Elisabeth looked at her daughter with some exasperation. "You aren't fit. You'd keel over from lack of sleep and sheer exhaustion after all that climbing and carrying. No one's as indispensable as that, Theresa."

"I'll say," said Chester Lane from the doorway. "For instance, I'm here instead of at school, even if the Rector's away. I couldn't stand the rumours, so I came down. I knew you'd be ringing me, but wanted to see you for myself. So, give! And then, of course, you're going to bed. Your mother can dope you if necessary."

"She will not be needing any pills," said Trudi. "Murdoch is in safe hands. He might have been in the lake. As soon as her head reaches the pillow, she will be—how do you say it? Out to it."

And so it proved.

CHAPTER TEN

THERESA kept in touch with Murdoch's parents by long-distance phone calls. She chafed at the thought of the almost two hundred miles of gorge and highway between them, but it was probably for the best. Murdoch would be spared any more personal excitement.

Hetty said, "The head injuries were superficial — logs in the river, no real damage. Odd thing is that he can remember all of it except crawling up that bank. Memory's a funny thing, isn't it?"

In the pause Theresa found herself wondering if he would remember anything of their conversation in the hospital that night.

"You're right, Mrs. Gunn. I've got all that from Conrad. He sings Murdo's praises non-stop. They tackled it at exactly the same moment, tried to keep together, each got terrible cracks, got swept to the other bank, saw that that shingle bank was still partly there, and had to decide to trust themselves to the current, and aim for it. And it was so near the lake. They could never have scaled the cliffs the other side — quite impossible. And as the river was still rising, they would have been drowned.

"The boy almost didn't make it. Murdoch grabbed him, made a superhuman effort, and the next moment they were flung on to the shingle. And in that very moment of safety, a boulder being tumbled over and over got Conrad's leg. He just passed straight out. I think Murdoch must have thought the rest of the beach would disappear any moment and they'd have a better chance anyway of being spotted if they reached the top of the bluff. It was magnificent."

Mrs. Gunn said, "Murdoch sent you a message today. He said it's about time you wrote to him, ratifying a conversation you had the night he was in Ludwigtown Hospital. He added, 'That is, tell her, if I didn't just dream it.' Tessa," There was entreaty in her

173

voice that said as plain as plain: "Dare I hope, but . . . don't hurt my son any more!" Mrs. Gunn tried again, "Tessa, does it mean—?"

Theresa said, "Mrs. Gunn, as a mother you've a right to know. I've never stopped loving him. Something happened that made me think I must give him up. I didn't tell him why. I was too young, too proud, too foolish. I can't tell you why because it concerns someone else. But he's got a right to know why now, though not till he's well enough. I'll do nothing to retard his recovery. That night he regained consciousness just long enough to say he was sure I still loved him. I confessed I did. The engagement is about to be resumed. I promised him and I won't go back on it. Only I must wait till he's well."

Hetty said softly, "Oh, how glad I am, how glad! So will James be. Only a month ago he said so wistfully that you two are so right for each other he could bang your heads together for not realising it. He said there was no other girl he so desired for his son as Tess. I won't probe, dear. You say it concerns someone else, so better to keep it to yourselves. Theresa, it's nothing from which another quarrel could spring, is it?"

The sound of Theresa's laugh was full of lovely confidence. "No, I'm going to stick to him like a leech! Oh, Mrs. Gunn, just tell Murdoch I'm ratifying the conversation all right. But I'll wait till he comes home. I won't do it by letter."

Five days later she had one from him.

Darling, I'm very nearly fit again, but they say another week. Mother delivered her message, said, "I've no idea what it means, but that's it." Poor Mother, she has no poker-face. The way she was beaming when she entered this ward, I knew perfectly well she knew. I wormed it all out of her. I can't imagine what it is. Someone must have made mischief. I'd pick Geraldine. But I don't care what it is, you've got to tell me. And tell me *now*. By letter. Then when we meet again it will be a glad reunion, not a time of probing. I'm as scared as hell that once you know I'm fit and well, you won't be so candid. I'm terrified a quarrel might spring up out of it. Not that that matters. If I have to quarrel with you once a week for the rest of my life, I don't care, as long as you marry me. But I'd like it, from the time we meet again, to be all joy. No, this isn't a love-letter, *Liebling,* it's a plea, an ultimatum. Oh, if only I could come home now, today, this moment. But write. *Immediately.*

Murdo.

She was terrified to write, but she had to. She could set it down composedly on paper, exactly as it happened. Not have to see Murdoch look ashamed and sorry. Because at the end she was going to convince him with the power of words that it no longer mattered.

She retired to her little attic that night, and it took her three hours. She sent it registered mail. How she got through the hours after sending it, she didn't know. She taught, mechanically, correctly but like an automaton. Because how could she gauge his reaction?

When she got home on the Friday there was a letter for her. From Murdoch. But how quick . . . and how thin it was. She knew apprehension, slit it open, realised he hadn't got hers when he had written this. But he would have it by now.

I'll be home Saturday. I've got a good clearance. No strain to be put on the leg yet, but that's purely precautionary. Hope I get your letter before I leave telling me your real reason for dumping me. Not that it matters. Mother and Father are driving me up — they aim to drop me at the Rectory at four. I want you there, waiting for me in my study. I want you to be wearing my ring as you promised, because whatever you tell me in that letter, Maria Theresa Keith, you small bad girl, whatever you had done or not done, it won't make any difference. We're engaged again and we'll be married as soon as school closes down in December. Oh, Tess, it was worth it all . . . every stroke of that swim in the River of the Whirlpool . . . because it brought

175

you back to me. No time for more. A nurse with no idea at all of what this letter means is waiting impatiently to post it for me. Love, Murdoch.

Theresa knew a blend of pain and joy that was almost unbearable. He thought it was something she had done. Oh, if only it had been just some foolish lovers' quarrel that had parted them, not this. If only the shadows of yesteryear did not cloud their happiness now.

She must banish it from her mind, meet tomorrow with delight, not regret.

She thought the hours of Saturday would never pass. Once noon had come and gone it wasn't so bad. Such a golden noon, even though this morning the Remarkables had been completely blotted out with mist.

After lunch she prowled. Four o'clock was so far away. She decided to go for a walk along the edge of the Lake of the Kingfisher. She had bought herself a new frock, in the colour Murdo liked best on her, vivid light green. It was a crimplene pinafore with a long bodice ending in box pleats and beneath it was a white blouse, collared, with a big white pussycat bow of muslin. The sleeves were full and caught into the wrist with yellow and red and black braid, giving it a faintly Austrian air. It was as near as she could get to the dress she had worn when Murdoch had proposed to her nearly three years ago.

She brushed her shoulder-length hair till it shone like spungold in the light from her window under the eaves. She liked it slightly longer like this. Her eyes looked like the stones under the waters of a brook, glinting brown and green in the sunlight. Happiness shone round her like an aura. Only one shadow remained. But she wouldn't let it show.

At that moment Doctor Riesdahl came briskly out of Anita's gate. He almost cannoned into her. "Oh, hullo, Theresa. I believe Murdoch's coming home today. Tell me, is it on?"

Her smile lit up her whole face, brought the dimple into display. "It is. We have a rendezvous at four in his study. I didn't come to see you about my problem

176

after all, doctor, because I decided the past was as dead as a dodo." She hesitated. "Nobody ill at Anita's, is there? Or shouldn't I ask? But I teach Murray and I'm very fond of him."

"No, just one of my routine checks on Inez. Don't usually do such things on Saturdays, but I was across at the house opposite. But Inez hasn't had an attack for some time now. Anita is wonderful with her, of course, and I've every hope she'll grow out of it."

"An attack of what? Is it all right to ask?"

"Asthma. We knew there'd be a tendency, of course. After all, her mother died of it. But it's very slight."

The next moment he was saying, "Theresa, what on earth are you boggling at?"

She said, trying to recover, "You said her mother died of it. Isn't she Anita's child?"

He boggled in turn. "No, of course not. She's her niece. Or, more correctly, Nort's niece — his sister's child. Actually, though, she's the dead spit of her father. It was very sad. He was killed just before the child was born. She was premature, due to the shock. And the mother never picked up, was always asthmatic and succumbed to an attack. Anita was a brick. So was Nort. They worship that child. All the children do too. She caught up and passed most fulltime babies. Well, I must move on. Give my regards and congratulations to Murdoch. I'll drop in later tonight — about nine — to look him over. I daresay he's got some tomfool notion of taking up the reins on Monday."

"I expect so. I doubt if we'll be able to hold him back."

The doctor went on, got in his car. He saw she was turning into Anita's gate. She'd suddenly looked like a room with all the lights turned on. But why?

Theresa hardly knew why she was doing this. There had been something — yes, there had to have been. She couldn't doubt the evidence of her own eyes, but at least it wasn't as bad as she'd thought. Oh, thank heaven she'd only mentioned "your affair with Anita" and had left out any reference to the child!

Anita saw her through the kitchen window, waved her in. As Theresa entered Anita said, "Oh, how beautiful you look—" She paused, said shrewdly, "Oh, you look as if someone has handed you the world on a golden platter. Ah . . . is Murdoch coming home soon?"

"Yes, this afternoon at four."

"No wonder you look like that. Is it on again? It must be. Nothing else could make you shine like that. I wondered — all that rescuing. Nothing brings two people together as much as trouble, I know."

Theresa nodded, her eyes ashine. "That's it, Anita." She turned to the neighbour. "If you wouldn't mind not telling the children till it's official. I don't know when Murdoch will announce it. I'll let you know when he does."

Julia dropped to a chair. "I won't breathe a word. One hint of this and young Susan would be out of the door, shrieking like the Town Crier on her way to tell her friends. All the kids at the school have been having bets on it, you know, as to how long it would take for you and the Rector to make it up again. And do call me Julia. I'm so thrilled. Nobody could be finer than Murdoch Gunn. I'll never forget—"

She stopped dead, looked apologetically at Anita. Anita said calmly, "I think Theresa should know what a fine husband she's getting. I told Murdoch he could tell you at the time, but he said these things have a habit of leaking out, and for Murray's sake, he didn't want that, and if he didn't tell you, at least you couldn't be blamed if it got out."

Theresa was staring at her in mystified fashion, but with hope.

Anita went on, "After Nort left me, I had some real trouble with Murray. It was all due to his being psychologically upset about his father. He knew enough about our quarrelling—he'd overheard a bit—to realise it was mostly my fault, and he resented it. On the surface he appeared as biddable as ever, but he was not going to the different clubs and things he said he was, at night. He got in with a wild lot.

"I was terribly glad Murdoch was teaching at Queenstown and living in his parents' cottage. He and I had always been good pals, you know, and he called round one or twice to see how I was making out. He saw Murray one night where he'd no business to be. He pulled no punches with Murray, made him own up to it. Spent hours and hours here two or three nights running. Then came an awful night when Murray went missing. I thought he'd run away.

"Murdoch had different ideas. He reckoned what he'd said to Murray had pulled him up, and thought, from something Murray had said, of what he wished he could do, that he'd gone to Dunedin to find his father, probably hitch-hiking. He rang the police at Roxburgh — they missed him there, but stopped a truck at Lawrence. They found him in it all right, and Murdoch left here, went down, collected him, brought him back, and talked sense into him till dawn.

"More than that, he came back later, had a talk with me, and made me think things out much more revealingly than I'd had the courage to do. And helped me compose a letter to Nort saying I was sorry for my bossy ways."

"Bossy ways!" repeated Theresa strangely.

The phone rang — Julia's husband. A visitor had arrived. Julia left, saying not to forget to let her know when it was official.

Theresa said to Anita, "You said bossy behaviour. Doesn't sound a very good reason for a husband leaving you."

Anita said slowly, "It was what it did to Nort that made it into a big thing, something he couldn't bear a moment longer. I was as blind as a bat — a perfectionist, an organiser. I didn't realise it, I thought I was the perfect helpmeet for Mort. I didn't realise I was swamping his personality. I was sapping his initiative, usurping his place as head of the family. I was terribly impatient with him, and he found it very belittling. His mother had done the same thing to him. He was lower-geared than I was, didn't have ambition;

I had too much. He had his own pace. I came to see that if he had married someone else, he'd have assumed his rightful place. He needed someone to be a clinging vine, and he'd have become strong.

"I even thought when he left that I'd show him I could make a jolly fine job of bringing up my family single-handed. And I couldn't. I became aware that even if I'd been in the habit of making the decisions, it had been Nort's more gentle, persuasive influence that had made the children happy, had made them want to obey. I didn't get him back right away. He'd gone to Australia. That letter chased him from town to town. I told him I was making a frightful job of bringing up the children alone, that I couldn't live without him. But he made me go to Dunedin to meet him. I had to go to him, he wouldn't come back to me." She laughed. "I liked that — respected him. But that terrible week when Murdoch stood by me, and the weeks after when I thought Nort wasn't going to answer my letter, I'll never forget. I'm so thrilled he's going to find all he's ever wanted with you, now. He used to come round here and talk about you. I longed to write and tell you what you were doing to him, but then I thought you were going to marry Rudi."

Theresa stood up. "Oh, Anita, thank you for telling me this. I can't explain why, but it's done something for me. Murdoch and I got our relationship into a snarl too—and it was my fault. Mine and someone else's. Someone who made mischief. I can't say more than that. But just lately I've found it wasn't true. That's why it's on again."

She couldn't say more than that. It would sadden Anita terribly if she as much as suspected Murdo's long-ago chivalry to her had wrecked his engagement. The old adages were so often right. Least said, soonest mended.

But none of this mattered. What did was that out of sheer, blind ignorance, she had blundered. Oh, if only she had waited till he came! How ironic she should find out just too late.

The next two hours were going to be sheer agony. Blindly, Theresa walked on up to the Rectory. She composed her face before she knocked on the door. Martha said, "Oh, come in, Theresa. The Rector rang me from Dunedin yesterday. He said he'd be here at four in the study and that you would be waiting for him. I'm aiming for a six-thirty dinner. Will that suit you both, do you think?"

Theresa tried to appear natural. "I think that would be just right, Martha, thank you very much."

Martha looked knowing. "I'm to have it all ready to serve, then I'm going over to your granny's. I'm having mine with her and spending the whole evening there."

She paused, said "It *is* on again, isn't it?"

Another of them!

Then, "Yes," said Theresa firmly. "It's on again, and this time for keeps. We're getting married in December. I'm going into the study right now for my ring. It's in his desk. He told me I was to be wearing it when we met again. But, Martha, I've got so much time to fill in. I'm going for a walk round by Ita-whakaata. I'll be back by half-past three, ready and waiting."

It did Theresa good. She felt about ten again, when things were always falling awry and Murdoch spent his time either fishing her out, or putting the pieces together again. He'd do it this time. He'd think it was just muddle-headed Theresa whom he loved, he didn't know why, and she'd got things wrong as usual.

A thought struck her. "Martha, when he does come, you won't let anyone interrupt us, will you? Not a parent, or a pupil, or anyone!"

"Over my dead body," warned Martha. "Honey, by the way, don't worry about me and this housekeeping job, or your granny living alone. I'll go over and live with her when you're wed."

Theresa took Martha's lined face between her cool young hands and dropped a kiss on her forehead. "Oh, Martha, you and Trudi are the salt of the earth," and went out of the room.

The Lake-of-the-little-reflections lay much as it had

lain on that other day except that now the poplars and the oaks were dressed in enamelled green, not gold, and instead of the asters, there were buttercups in the grass and red clover . . . but once more it was a day of stillness, so that the Hereford cattle and the Romney sheep were twin reflections as they wound their way round the edge of the lake. The weeping willows trailed lacy fingers in the water and surely they were the self-same geese, setting out in single file from the other shore, looking like the carved prows of alabaster boats. Back in the gully *tuis* were twanging their woodland harps, and up in the sky a lark so high it couldn't be seen was singing its heart out. A cricket chirped in the grass. Above the water's edge a dragonfly hung poised, glinting green and bronze, gauzy wings aglitter. On a dead blue-gum branch sticking out of the water, the kingfisher waited, striking a note of turquoise and green.

Theresa looked down at the emerald on her finger. Now she felt complete again with its weight on her finger. If only, if only she knew how Murdoch had taken her letter. What a hideous mistake! If only this last hour would pass. She looked down and saw her own reflection, a deeper green in the waters of the lake. Green and white.

Then she heard it. Her name. In the voice she loved best in all the world, just as she had heard it that August day on the Kapuzinerberg. No, not just the same. That one had been a little tentative.

This wasn't. It wasn't tentative, or angry, or for-bearing or — it was just full of gladness.

She turned round, her hands clasped in front of her, to still their trembling, and the big emerald flashed fire in the sun. Murdo was positively charging down the track, no sign of a limp.

He was still saying it, "Theresa . . . Maria Theresa . . . Tess!"

Her poem was still as true as it had ever been. No one *had* ever said her name as Murdoch had said it. Her eyes dazzled with sheer joy.

He almost reached her, then checked, looking at her as if he would never be done looking. She said, in a wondering tone, "You *aren't* angry? Murdo, I just found out today, that there was nothing to it. That Julia Balmoral was there all that night. That you were helping Anita with Murray. Oh, can you ever forgive me?"

She put out two hands, and he took them. There was a look in his eyes she had never seen there before. "Theresa, you were willing to forgive me *that*? I can see how it was. Thank goodness you know. I was coming to find you, to tell you. I didn't get your letter till late yesterday afternoon. I'd been discharged in the morning and they rang to say a registered letter was there for me. I wanted to come up right away. I didn't dare phone you — not safe enough — and if I'd come up you might have been in bed. And the doctor said he'd rather I didn't drive myself up anyway.

"So we set off earlier this morning. I was going to shake you till your teeth rattled first, then haul you round to Anita to get her to tell you the truth. Thank heaven we don't have to!"

He stopped, said, "Tess, my love, can you believe it . . . this is the first time in more than two years that we've met without fighting? Well . . . what are you waiting for? I told you that morning on the Kapuzinerberg that one proposal was enough for a lifetime, and that was all you were ever going to have!"

So it was up to her. She took that one step forward, said, "Oh, Murdo! Murdo!" lifted up her arms and was received into his hungry embrace.

Theresa didn't care if it went on for ever. Nothing of the angry possession of his kiss that night they went to the Mirabell Gardens was in this. This was a giving and a covenant. It lasted a long time.

Murdoch lifted his head. The side of his mouth quirked up in the old familiar way. His eyes, as always at times of great emotion, were almost black, not red-brown. "Theresa, I could skin you! If only you'd put your ring on that day in Salzburg, we could have honey-

183

mooned in Heiligenblut. We needn't have wasted any more time. We could have toured Europe together, explored London, done all the things we always dreamed of doing, and now, you small bad girl, what can we do?"

He pulled her down to the edge of the little track facing the beauty of the gentian blue lake. He kissed her again. "Well, now you've admitted you love me, I'll tell you what we are going to do! School breaks up on the eighth of December this year. We get married on the sixteenth and on the eighteenth we fly to Europe. I booked it by telephone from the hospital. We'll celebrate Weihnachten with Tante Evelina and Uncle Ernst in Salzburg and the New Year will find us in Heiligenblut for our honeymoon. I absolutely refuse to let you cheat us out of all our dreams! Oh, if you keep on looking starry-eyed like that I'll have to keep on kissing you." He leaned over her.

In between he reproached her for the dance she had led him. "The things you made me do . . . I tried to provoke you by saying I'd thought of selling the ring in London, I entered into a mighty conspiracy with half Ludwigtown and all your family to get you here; I nearly got bowled out when Rudi arrived and I had to make faces at him so he wouldn't let on Trudi was as well as ever. Phew! I've written to Geraldine, by the way, to say the game's up. I thought it would upset you too much to do it. I've told her not to bother writing and trying to make us believe she did it in good faith. She'll know why it would never convince me. She was jealous of you, Tess.

"Oh, if only I'd had any suspicion — at first — that she might have made mischief. Later, you know, after you'd been gone a year, she thought she might console me, but didn't meet with any success. I'd not realised she was in Canada and not too far away from where I was staying, either. But she heard about it from someone here and came across to see me."

Theresa said, "Oh, Mother said you'd gone to see her." She dimpled. "I was jealous!"

He burst out laughing. "I only gave her a quarter of an hour. I never could stand her — she was sneaky. And she played on your sympathies even as a child. I rang Catriona, who, good sport as she is, caught on. I pretended, in front of Geraldine, that I had another appointment, said I was sorry, but I'd be ten minutes or so late. I took Geraldine to the door, and parted with her there and then. But, Jove, Maria Theresa, you gave me some bad moments in Salzburg, keeping up the pretence that I was staying on in Europe. I was just dying to see you off to Munich and on your way. I was terrified someone from Ludwigtown would write and blow the news about my appointment. Perhaps it was bigheaded of me, but I had a feeling that if only we could have long enough together in Ludwigtown, our own place, our coming together would be inevitable."

Theresa snuggled her head into his shoulder in an ecstasy of happiness. She felt she could just stay here for hours.

Murdoch heaved a mock sigh, said, "It'll be no sort of preparation for a wedding. We'll be as busy as hell right up to that last week. Trust you! I can't spare you from my staff till the very day we break up. Can you imagine it? In two weeks' time we'll be right into school exams, University Entrance Exams, bursaries, reports, the practices for the prize-giving, the Leavers' Ball. It's going to be nothing but school, school, school! This will probably be the last uninterrupted evening we'll have till then!"

Theresa had raised herself up on her elbow and was looking over his shoulder. "We aren't going to have even that," she said.

The Rector sat bolt upright, took one horrified look, groaned. There they came, a string of First and Second Formers up from the Lake's edge beyond a clump of willows. They all carried fish dangling from their fingers. Not one of them had a rod!

The Rector said to his fiancée, "Just look at them! Why the hell didn't they stay hidden? Then I wouldn't have known they'd been guddling trout! Now I shall have to read them a lecture, and I never felt less like being severe with anyone!"

"It's extremely noble of them," said Theresa, who had had longer to observe them. "They're going to risk having the vials of your wrath poured out on their heads. They're boys with consciences. Don't you see, Murdo? They've *had* to show up. See . . . the ones at the back are supporting Philip. He's got a bleeding nose."

Philip, two handkerchiefs clutched to his nose, looked up at his Rector and mumbled, "Sorry, sir. We saw you coming and we ducked down. I hit the willow branch."

The Rector said sternly, "Ha! Guilty consciences, eh? Not one of you has a rod!"

By now Philip was a horrifying sight, but he was game to the end. "Oh, no sir," he said virtuously, "we just didn't want to spoil your fun, that's all."

Theresa saw the Rector blush pinkly for the first time ever. She felt a giggle coming on and clapped her hands to her mouth to stifle it. They all saw it at once—the emerald. They all said: "Ahhhhhhhhh!" in tones of deepest satisfaction.

She held out her hand. "In the words of half of Ludwigtown, it's on again!" she said. "Look, I'll use my influence to get him to let you off about the fish, but you'd better say your prayers backwards that we don't meet the river ranger!"

The Rector said grimly. "One thing I'm adamant on. You can all earn money these days in holidays and after school. You must get rods and licences if you want to fish."

Spike Lenham said, "Sir, we have. Rods and licences. Only it's such fun to see if you catch them with your bare hands."

The Rector had difficulty keeping his face straight. "Yes, I know — at least I imagine so — but you must keep within the law. Understood?"

"Yes, sir." It was a chorus.

Murdoch said, "Well, I'll let you off on one condi-

tion only . . . that is that you don't describe the—er—
scene you've just witnessed in detail at school on Monday morning!"

Another chorus, this time of chagrin. The Rector
burst out laughing. "All right. But it was a good try.
About as effective as King Canute trying to keep the
tide back. I bow to the inevitable."

They looked impressed. That was handsome of the
Head. Something must be done in return. Clive Whitley
said, "If it's any comfort to you, sir, we could only *see*.
We couldn't hear a thing!"

Theresa's eyes met Murdoch's. That was something
to be thankful for.

Murdoch, much relieved, said, "You'd better come
to the Rectory, because Philip's nose is going to take
some stopping. Besides—" He stopped.

Theresa finished it, her eyes dancing. "Besides, the
path to the Rectory is a private one. Not so much
chance of meeting the ranger."

The Rector added, "But keep those fish behind your
back anyway. And if you don't push your luck too
far, I have a feeling your future Rector's wife might
even cook them for you."

Clive coughed. "Sir, we have someone else with us.
She thought she'd better lie low, but she caught two
of them. Do you think—?"

Theresa knew it. She knew it in her bones. She said
limply, "Brenda? It would have to be Brenda."

They nodded. "She's beaut at it. She showed us how."
They turned, called, "You can come out. It's okay."

Theresa saw the blood was getting out of hand again
after a temporary check. She tore into two halves her
best handkerchief, said, "Philip, I'll plug your
nose, I'm afraid," and proceeded to do so.

Brenda, in indescribable jeans covered with fish
scales and — it must be admitted — guts, emerged
from the willows. She wore the look of one who has
engineered it all even if it isn't likely she'll get the
credit.

Martha's face was a study when she beheld them.

"Well, I never! I thought you were going to—" she bit it off.

Jacky Moore looked up, his freckled face naïve and pleased. "Oh, he did, Mrs. Hallows. We were all witnesses!"

Murdoch got some ice-blocks out of the fridge, managed to stop the bleeding. The boys gutted the fish that hadn't been done. Martha and Theresa fried them. They all sat down at the big kitchen table to eat them. Martha too.

Finally the boys and Brenda departed. Martha closed the door. "Now I'll get a scarf over my head and be away. It's all ready for you. Good job I didn't do an entrée. You sitting down with your pupils eating poached trout! Wait till I tell Trudi, she'll never believe it!"

At last, blessedly, they were alone.

They went through hand-in-hand, opened the door. The fire was a steady glow. A big chair was drawn close. A small round table was draped with a lace cloth and a tiny bowl on it held anemones, so reminiscent of those on the Austrian hillsides. The drapes were drawn and Martha must have put a match to the candles before she left.

The silver winked in the firelight, a bottle of champagne stood in its bucket. The napkins were snowy, the crystal goblets winking back the purples and pinks of the anemones.

"Only one thing left to make it perfect," said Murdoch, smiling.

"What could that be?" wondered Theresa.

"This," said Murdoch, and took the phone off the hook.

He turned to her and held out his arms.

F R E E ! ! !

Did you know . . . . . ?

that just by mailing in the coupon below you can re-
ceive a brand new, up-to-date "Harlequin Romance
Catalogue" listing literally hundreds of Harlequin Romances you probably thought were out of print.

Now you can shop in your own home for novels by
your favorite Harlequin authors — the Essie Summers
you wanted to read, the Violet Winspear you missed,
the Mary Burchell you thought wasn't available any-
more!

They're all listed in the "Harlequin Romance Catalogue". And something else too — the books are listed
in numerical sequence, — so you can fill in the missing
numbers in your library.

Don't delay — mail the coupon below to us today.
We'll promptly send you the "Harlequin Romance
Catalogue".

PLEASE NOTE: Harlequin Romance Catalogue of available titles is revised every
three months.

FREE!

TO: **HARLEQUIN READER SERVICE, Dept. N 506**
M.P.O. Box 707, Niagara Falls, N.Y. 14302
Canadian address: Stratford, Ont., Canada

☐ Please send me the free Harlequin Romance Catalogue.
☐ Please send me the titles checked.

I enclose $_____ (No C.O.D.'s). All books listed are 60c
each. To help defray postage and handling cost, please add 25c.

Name _____

Address _____

City/Town _____

State/Prov. _____ Zip _____

Have You Missed Any of These
Harlequin Romances?

PLEASE NOTE: All Harlequin Romances from #1857 onwards are 75c. Books below that number, where available are priced at 60c through Harlequin Reader Service until December 31st, 1975.

AA

Have You Missed Any of These Harlequin Romances?

- [ ] 941 MAYENGA FARM
      Kathryn Blair
- [ ] 945 DOCTOR SANDY
      Margaret Malcolm
- [ ] 948 ISLANDS OF SUMMER
      Anne Weale
- [ ] 951 THE ENCHANTED TRAP
      Kate Starr
- [ ] 957 NO LEGACY FOR LINDSAY
      Essie Summers
- [ ] 965 CAME A STRANGER
      Celine Conway
- [ ] 968 SWEET BRENDA
      Penelope Walsh
- [ ] 974 NIGHT OF THE HURRICANE
      Andrea Blake
- [ ] 984 ISLAND IN THE DAWN
      Averil Ives
- [ ] 993 SEND FOR NURSE ALISON
      Marjorie Norrell
- [ ] 994 JUBILEE HOSPITAL
      Jan Tempest
- [ ] 1001 NO PLACE FOR SURGEONS
      Elizabeth Gilzean
- [ ] 1004 THE PATH OF THE
      MOONFISH, Betty Beaty
- [ ] 1009 NURSE AT FAIRCHILDS
      Marjorie Norrell
- [ ] 1010 DOCTOR OF RESEARCH
      Elizabeth Houghton
- [ ] 1011 THE TURQUOISE SEA
      Hilary Wilde
- [ ] 1018 HOSPITAL IN THE TROPICS
      Gladys Fullbrook
- [ ] 1019 FLOWER OF THE MORNING
      Celine Conway
- [ ] 1024 THE HOUSE OF DISCONTENT
      Esther Wyndham
- [ ] 1048 HIGH MASTER OF CLERE
      Jane Arbor
- [ ] 1052 MEANT FOR EACH OTHER
      Mary Burchell
- [ ] 1074 NEW SURGEON AT ST.
      LUCIAN'S, Elizabeth
      Houghton
- [ ] 1087 A HOME FOR JOCELYN
      Eleanor Farnes
- [ ] 1094 MY DARK RAPPAREE
      Henrietta Reid

- [ ] 1098 THE UNCHARTED OCEAN
      Margaret Malcolm
- [ ] 1102 A QUALITY OF MAGIC
      Rose Burghely
- [ ] 1106 WELCOME TO PARADISE
      Jill Tahourdin
- [ ] 1115 THE ROMANTIC HEART
      Norrey Ford
- [ ] 1120 HEART IN HAND
      Margaret Malcolm
- [ ] 1121 TEAM DOCTOR, Ann Gilmour
- [ ] 1122 WHISTLE AND I'LL COME
      Flora Kidd
- [ ] 1138 LOVING IS GIVING
      Mary Burchell
- [ ] 1144 THE TRUANT BRIDE
      Sara Seale
- [ ] 1150 THE BRIDE OF MINGALAY
      Jean S. Macleod
- [ ] 1166 DOLAN OF SUGAR HILLS
      Kate Starr
- [ ] 1172 LET LOVE ABIDE
      Norrey Ford
- [ ] 1182 GOLDEN APPLE ISLAND
      Jane Arbor
- [ ] 1183 NEVER CALL IT LOVING
      Marjorie Lewty
- [ ] 1184 THE HOUSE OF OLIVER
      Jean S. Macleod
- [ ] 1200 SATIN FOR THE BRIDE
      Kate Starr
- [ ] 1201 THE ROMANTIC DR. RYDON
      Anne Durham
- [ ] 1209 THE STUBBORN DR STEPHEN
      Elizabeth Houghton
- [ ] 1211 BRIDE OF KYLSAIG
      Iris Danbury
- [ ] 1214 THE MARSHALL FAMILY
      Mary Burchell
- [ ] 1216 ORANGES AND LEMONS
      Isobel Chace
- [ ] 1218 BEGGARS MAY SING
      Sara Seale
- [ ] 1222 DARK CONFESSOR
      Elinor Davis
- [ ] 1236 JEMIMA
      Leonora Starr

PLEASE NOTE: All Harlequin Romances from #1857 onwards are 75c. Books below that number, where available are priced at 60c through Harlequin Reader Service until December 31st, 1975.

BB

Have You Missed Any of These Harlequin Romances?

PLEASE NOTE: All Harlequin Romances from #1857 onwards are 75c. Books below that number, where available are priced at 60c through Harlequin Reader Service until December 31st, 1975.

CC